POACHER TO
KING'S KNIGHT

POACHER TO KING'S KNIGHT

WILLIAM MARPLES

authorHOUSE®

AuthorHouse™ UK Ltd.
1663 Liberty Drive
Bloomington, IN 47403 USA
www.authorhouse.co.uk
Phone: 0800.197.4150

Published by AuthorHouse   10/02/2013

ISBN: 978-1-4918-8070-8 (sc)
ISBN: 978-1-4918-8071-5 (e)

PREAMBLE

THIS STORY IS complete fiction. Set in 12th Century England, a grey area in English history known as the Period of Anarchy, when Barons, Lords, and Bishops each had their own knight's and soldiers. Fighting between each other to gain land and with it power. This was a brutal, cruel and violent time where life itself had little value.

It was a beautiful late summer evening, the villager's of Farnsfield were making their way to the church, situated at the edge of their village located in a great forest called Sherwood. Children's laughter filled the air as they danced down the road with their parents. When a hush came over the village, children fell quiet and the birds stopped singing. In the distance a low thunder like rumble was heard, but there were no clouds in the sky. The rumble became louder and louder each second. The villager's stood rooted to the spot, clasping their children close to them. A large company of soldiers appeared from out of the forest, their horse's hooves thundering on the hard dry earth. At the command of their leader, they began to herd the people into a circle, brutally prodding them with their lances, anyone who tried to flee were immediately struck down and killed without mercy including the women and children. The leader stopped outside the church, watching these violent proceedings. When from the church a knight accompanied by the priest, who on hearing the screams outside had come to see what was happening. The knight strode toward the leader of the soldier's.

"What in God's name is going on here?" he yelled. "Who are you, what do you want here?"

"Are you the Lord of this Manor?" asked the Soldier.

"Yes I am." The knight answered.

"In the King's name, I accuse you of treason and treachery against the King. You are hereby stripped of your land and titles and sentenced to death," then calling to his men, "Drive him back into the church." Facing these great odds and being unarmed the knight was driven back into the church. "Block the entrance to the building so no one escapes, then bring torches, kill everyone I want no witnesses." The slaughter continued until every man, woman and child they could find were dead. Torches were lit and one was given to the Baron, who immediately hurled it onto the church roof. The soldiers followed suit setting the church on fire, ignoring the screams of the people inside. The Baron had gained one more estate and one more morsel of power.

ACKNOWLEDGEMENTS

My thanks to Kathryn Smith for proof reading my story, and to my long suffering wife Carol, without whose help and encouragement I would never have had this book published. And not forgetting the girls at the Dovecote Café, for keeping me supplied with mugs of tea.

Cover and Illustrations by James Fraser

CHAPTER ONE

THE SOUND OF a horse pulling a cart being driven hard, then suddenly coming to an abrupt halt close to where Toby the young poacher was repairing the inside of his shelter, caused him to stop what he was doing and listen. He could hear voices and wondered why anyone would stop so deep into Sherwood. The slightest sound carried a long way in the quiet of the forest; he listened carefully, and could just make out a man's voice,

"Get out here and hide. I will try to draw Osbert's men as far away as I can, but this workhorse can't outrun their mounts. Wait awhile, and then try to get to the village of Ravenshead. Look for the priest there; he has no love for Osbert, he will tend your wounds and hide you until you are able to go on your way. I will try to return there when they have given up the hunt," a second voice replied.

"Look to yourself Thomas, they will never give up the hunt, and if they catch you they will kill you. You know that to be true. Don't come back to look for us, we will make our own way north, I have friends there. If we make it o'er the River Don, then we will be safe. May good fortune follow you Thomas, and thank you my friend."

"Aye, very well Sire," Thomas soulfully replied, then added, "Take care Miss Rebecca, it's a long way to the Don from here even for an able man. Look to your father for he is sorely wounded and needs help to tend his wounds."

"Thank you, I will. Go now quickly before they catch up to you," Rebecca answered.

"Aye. Move on," called Thomas as he whipped the horse into a gallop taking the cart on its way again at high speed.

Toby was a tall, sturdily built youth for his fifteen years, with light brown hair and dressed like a woodsman, with the exception of his sleeveless jacket, which was fashioned from rabbit skins, his trademark when selling his wares. He crawled out of his shelter, one of many he had made in Sherwood Forest during the last three years, to use when he was working as a rabbit catcher and poacher in the area. They were easily made, usually under an old hawthorn hedge or bush and were thatched with straw or bracken on the inside to keep out the wind and rain. The floor covered with sacks of bracken for a bed, (when he could find the sacks,) if not, just bracken. To get inside he crawled through a small tunnel—like opening. They were dry when the weather was wet and to anyone passing by, could not be distinguished from the normal hedgerow. To Toby these shelters were his refuge and home while he was in the area.

While keeping out of sight, Toby curiously looked about him, looking for whoever had been called Sire and the other a female. The breaking of twigs and loud rustling noises told him the couple were coming toward him and would be entering a small clearing directly in front of him. When they appeared, Toby saw a man of average height, but stocky in build, dressed as you would see a man of noble birth, carrying a sheathed sword in his left hand, but using it as you would a walking stick. He was stumbling and falling to the ground with the female Rebecca, a young slim girl with long mousey coloured hair, well dressed of about fourteen years old trying desperately to hold him up, and then falling alongside him. Toby could clearly see the blood stained bandage wrapped around the man's left thigh. Rebecca rose and tried desperately to lift the nobleman to his feet.

"Come father," she urged, "we must get away from the road or they will surely find us. You must help me, I cannot lift you myself you are too heavy for me."

The Nobleman leant on his sword, and with the aid of his daughter, struggled to raise himself to his feet. Without making a sound, Toby came upon them as if from nowhere.

"Let me help you," Toby offered placing his shoulder under the Nobleman's armpit. "If you are travelling north, then you must go this way," he said pointing out the direction, "I can hide you tonight, but your daughter's right, you must get away from the road. You are leaving a trail a blind man could follow and making enough noise to wake the dead. Baron Osbert's men will be scouring the countryside looking for you."

"Who are you? Where did you come from? Why should you help us? Are you one of Osbert's men? How do we know you will not lead us to them?" Rebecca's questions came thick and fast.

"Do I look like one of Osbert's men dressed as I am? I am known as Toby the poacher to my friends and the villagers in this Shire. Let's get your father somewhere where he can rest awhile, and then I will answer all your questions," replied Toby. "But for now save your breath to help me get your father to safety, and keep quiet, voices travel a long way here in the forest. I have a place where you can hide tonight but it's quite a distance for a wounded man, or shall I just go on my way and forget I ever saw you?"

"Come now Rebecca," the nobleman interrupted, "I can't go on much longer, I must rest up and have my wounds tended. We must trust this young man, so be quiet and let's get on."

For the next two hours, Toby led them deeper into the forest, stopping occasionally to rest their aching limbs and for Toby to backtrack, to remove any tracks they had left that the soldiers could follow. At last they came on a clearing by a small stream.

"One last effort and we're there," declared Toby.

"Where?" asked Rebecca. "I do not see any buildings. Where is this place of yours? I hope the beds are soft, I'm tired and worn out."

"You see that clump of bushes by the stream," said Toby pointing across the clearing, "that's one of my shelters, and no, there are no beds apart from the bracken you will put on the floor. It's somewhere your father can rest and be safe for the night; a place the soldiers won't find you. They will search every building for miles around looking for you. When we get your father inside and comfortable, I will go on apiece. There is a village I know where I have friends. I will bring back food and clean dressings to wrap your father's wounds."

They crossed the clearing to the shelter. The nobleman half crawled and was half dragged inside the small entrance, which was only just large enough for a man to crawl through, followed by a loudly complaining Rebecca. There was not much room for the three of them inside, it was the length of three yards and the width of only two, and they had to crawl on their knees as it was only four feet at the highest point, there wasn't room to stand. "But I'm a La . . . , I'm not used to sleeping in a hedge like an animal. I'm tired and dirty, my dress is torn, I need to bathe and put on clean clothes!"

Rebecca protested. "You must find me something better than this"

"Baron Osbert's men wouldn't expect you to hide under a hedge either, that's the whole point. They could walk within feet of you and not know you are here. They will be searching every village, farm and farm building in the area to find you. They will be burning whole farms, beating men, women and children, some maybe to death, just to satisfy their brutality and frustration at not finding you. Believe me, I have seen it all before at the hands of Osbert and his men; bathe in the stream if you must, but try to keep out of sight," warned Toby.

"Rebecca. Oh Rebecca!" said her father, "please be quiet and think about our situation. The lad is doing his best for us. He makes sense, and think on by helping us he is putting his own life in danger. So please stop complaining, do as he says and help him. I can go no further this day," He then turned onto his back and slipped into a deep sleep. Toby moved to the entrance,

"Your father is weak, he's lost a lot of blood, let him sleep. Help me get fresh bedding, and then you too can rest while I go to the village." Rebecca followed Toby out of the shelter still complaining under her breath, begrudgingly, yet willing at last to help carry large bundles of fresh bracken back to the shelter.

"Go inside now and strew the bedding around to make it comfortable, and then get some rest yourself. You will be safe here. But don't come out again until I get back. There are foresters and woodsmen about; if they see a young girl out here, and a stranger to them, they will want to know who you are and why you are here. Word may get back to Baron Osbert's men. So for once, please do as you're asked or you will put both your own and your father's life in danger. Do you understand?"

"Yes I understand. Please hurry back. I do not like being in the forest at night. I've heard there are wild boar and great stags that will tear a man to pieces. With father injured and unable to defend us, I am afraid," pleaded Rebecca.

"Oh! You need me at last do you!" Toby grinned, "Cover your father with the bracken to keep him warm. I'll be back afore sunset, and don't worry; the wild animals only tear men to pieces, not little girls, they eat little girls whole! Block the entrance with bracken so they can't get in."

With that he turned and disappeared into the forest. Rebecca crawled into the shelter as fast as she could and, forgetting all about needing a bath, she stuffed the entrance full of bracken, then lay by her father's side and went off to sleep.

Toby made his way quickly through the forest, stopping occasionally to look and listen for danger as he headed toward the village of Glenford, a place he had known for most of his short life. A place that held both good and terrible memories for him, but now a place where he knew he could come to for help. He entered the village from a path behind the houses and made his way to a house near the centre of the village. The street was quiet and almost empty of people. All to the good he thought, he didn't want to be seen today. Most of the villagers would be out in the fields or in the forest working as usual, but not the person he had come to see. He banged his fist on the door frame calling.

"Granny Smith, are you there?"

"Yes I'm here, who wants me?" came the reply from within.

"It's me Toby," he answered.

"Who's there? Toby who?" she asked as she came to the door, "Oh! It's you Tobias, come in, I haven't set eyes on you for ages, where have you been? How are you keeping, are you looking after yourself? Silly question I can see you are, you look well. Have you a rabbit for me? I do like a bit of rabbit stew. Come and have a bite of bread with me, I have a little goat's cheese to go with it. Tell me what you've been doing with yourself all this time." She handed Toby a piece of bread with cheese, which he eagerly took and started to eat.

"No rabbit this time Granny, I've come to ask for your help as a healer," Toby started to explain.

"My goodness, are you hurt Tobias? Are you ill?" Granny asked.

"No, I am well and not hurt, it's not for me. I am helping a man of noble birth and his daughter to escape from Baron Osbert's thugs. The man is wounded and has lost a lot of blood, which makes him too weak to travel until he's rested and had his wound tended. I know you would be putting yourself in danger by helping, so I thought perhaps you could give me clean dressings and tell me how to clean and dress the wound. I would beg some food for them too. You know that I will repay you when I return. Please, will you help me?"

"Oh Tobias, what have you got yourself into, don't you know who it is you are helping?" Granny Smith put her hands to her face; tears welled up in her eyes as she continued. "We have heard of this in the village, the soldiers came looking, they won't stop until they have found him. It is Sir Simon de Selis; a friend to the Archbishop of York that you are aiding. Word is that he overheard Baron Osbert and his brother plotting with Robert the Earl of Gloucester, half brother to Empress Maud, to overthrow all the Lords, Barons and Bishops loyal to King Stephen. They mean to replace them with men loyal to Empress Maud, men who would support their cause and take control of all the lands in the north and build an army. If they could do this they would control over half of England and be in a position to take the throne from King Stephen. Gloucester, Osbert and other conspirators want to replace him with the King's cousin, the Empress Maud, to ensure Henry her son, who she claims is the rightful heir to the throne, is crowned king. Well an argument between Sir Simon de Selis and Baron Osbert ensued, in which Osbert's brother was slain. Sir Simon was lucky to escape with his life. His servant Thomas of Doncaster was caught, tortured and executed for the murder, but would not tell where his master was hiding. The priest at Ravenshead, Father Joseph, was accused of harbouring them and was also put to the sword. Leave well alone and go your own way Tobias, lest they find you with them and put you to the sword also. Mark my words; they are like dogs fighting over a bone, no good will come of it."

"I thought it must be something big for Baron Osbert to try to kill someone his equal," said Toby, "I would help anyone against that Norman butcher Baron Ralph Osbert. You remember what he did to my family? I know what he would do to me if ever he found me. Well this may be the chance I have been waiting for to clear my family's name, and to get revenge. I mean to help them more than ever now. If you don't want to get involved I will find another way, but I will help them. Just promise me that you won't tell anyone that you have seen me or what I am about and I'll be on my way."

"Oh you're just like your father, headstrong and stubborn. Give me time to put a few bits and pieces into a bag; a loaf of bread, butter and cheese, a jug of corn brew to warm them inside, a poultice and clean dressing for the wound, needle and twine, then I will come with you, to see for myself what you are getting us both into."

Granny Smith moved round the dwelling collecting these as she spoke. "I would never forgive myself if I didn't help you; besides I like the thought of revenge too."

"Thank you Granny!" Toby gave her a hug. "I promise you won't regret it."

"Aye that's as maybe, let's wait and see. I have your father's bow and arrows in the chest over there; they may come in useful, and a change of clothes to get you out of those rabbit skins. Come on, take the bag and don't drop it, let's go before the villagers get back asking questions, and before it gets too dark to see what I'm doing when we get to wherever you are taking me." Granny urged.

"These rabbit skins are a good disguise," said Toby, picking up the things he thought he may need with Granny's bag, "Everyone knows me as Toby the poacher or Toby the rabbit catcher, the coat is my trademark. The pockets inside carry my food and drink, it keeps me warm and dry. A lot of rabbits died to make this. It shows my customers I can deliver what I promise, but I will take some of the clothes and the bow. I may come back for the rest of father's things afore long."

They left Granny's house by the same path Toby had arrived, keeping to the hedgerows and under cover of the forest wherever they could. Granny wasn't very big but extremely nimble for her fifty six years, and easily kept up with Toby. They arrived at the clearing close to the shelter. Toby looked around, everything seemed to be alright but, just to make sure, he asked Granny to wait under cover, and then went on by himself. When he arrived at the shelter, he pushed aside the bracken, crawled through the entrance and went inside. The nobleman stirred, disturbed by the rustling as Toby entered. Rebecca was still sleeping soundly.

"It's me Toby, are you awake?"

"Aye, just about," the nobleman turned to his daughter, "Rebecca, rouse yourself, Toby's back from the village."

"I've brought a little food and someone to tend your wounds," Toby told him, "I'll bring her to you." He turned and crawled back out of the shelter and headed across the clearing to where Granny Smith was waiting. Collecting the bag and their belongings, he beckoned her to follow him back to the shelter. When they were all inside Toby spoke,

"This is Granny Smith. She is a healer from the village and is here to tend your wound; she has also brought you a little food and a drop of corn brew. I have brought a fresh doublet and hose for you to change into. I will destroy the blooded ones you are wearing later."

"There's not much room in here with the four of us," Granny observed. "Tobias, take the girl out while I take a look at her father's leg, I will call if I need anything." Rebecca looked alarmingly toward her father.

"Go on," he assured her, "I will be in good hands I think." Rebecca followed Toby outside.

"Right Sir Simon de Selis," said Granny, "let's take a look at this leg of yours."

"You know who I am?" Sir Simon asked, "If so then you know what would happen to you, if you are caught helping me."

"Yes I know who you are, and why you are being hunted. I also know that Thomas your servant was tortured and put to the sword along with the priest at Ravenshead and yes I know the penalty I would pay if we are caught. Just lie still while I take a look here." Granny slowly removed the dressing and cut his hose back to get to the wound.

"Here take a sip of this," she handed him the corn brew, "Just a sip mind, I need some of it to clean this wound as it has cleansing and healing powers you understand," she uncovered the wound, "I will clean it, stitch the open flesh back together and put on a poultice to stop it festering. Then it can be redressed. Leave the poultice on tonight, I will return on the morrow to change it."

All the time she was talking she was bathing and cleaning the wound. "The wound is deep but will heal. The loss of blood is the reason you are weak. You may want to rest up another day or two to get your strength back, then with care you should be able to travel."

"Just to say thank you for what you are doing is not enough. If you know me you will know I speak the truth when I tell you I will find a way to repay both you and Toby for your help," Sir Simon raised himself on his elbow, "but I cannot understand why you should both risk your lives for us."

"Tobias must speak for himself; but I have more reason to hate Baron Osbert than you my Lord, let that suffice for now," Granny told him. "There that's done, it should feel better now. It will be stiff and painful for awhile, but you are a strong man and should heal well. My work is finished here; I must find Tobias and say my goodbyes. Goodbye to you my Lord. I will tend you again tomorrow."

"Thank you again Granny Smith, I won't forget your kindness," replied Sir Simon, but Granny was already on her way through to the outside.

Meanwhile Toby had taken Rebecca away from the shelter and down to the stream; he could see how nervous she was by the way she was continually looking back to the shelter.

"Your father Sir Simon de Selis is in good hands. Don't worry they will call if they need us." Toby assured her.

"Who is that woman? Can we trust her? How do we know she will not go straight to Baron Osbert when she leaves here? How do I know she is not doing harm to my father right now? We only have your word on the matter. I am still not sure I trust you either." Rebecca stopped suddenly and turned to Toby, "How do you know who we are, we have not told you? . . . Baron Osbert must have told you . . . Why you treacherous dog, you mean to turn us over to him for blood money!" she cried, hurling herself toward him with flailing fists.

"Whoa!" cried Toby grabbing her by both wrists. Rebecca struggled to get free, kicking out with her feet at Toby's legs, "Whoa," he called again, "listen to me, let me explain will you?" Toby was a strong, well made boy for his fifteen years, and could easily hold her at arm's length. When she realised struggling was hopeless, Rebecca stood quiet.

"Go on, explain," she said, "but do not expect me to believe a word you say. Let me go, I know you can overpower me I will not attack you again."

Toby felt her arms relax.

"Good, now be quiet and listen. I know because word came to the village that Baron Osbert's brother had been murdered, and that Sir Simon de Selis and his henchmen were the culprits. Anyone even suspected of giving you succour will be put to death. Thomas of Doncaster and the priest at Ravenshead have already been tortured and killed."

Rebecca gasped and put her hand to her mouth as if to stifle a cry, as she realised that Toby was telling her the truth.

"Has my father been informed of this? Thomas is . . . was a good servant and friend. And why kill the priest? He was not there; he has given us no help."

"By now Granny Smith will have told your father. As for the priest, I'm afraid you will have to see into the past

≈ 13 ≈

to answer that. And Granny Smith well, she like me has reason to hate Baron Osbert more than you or your father. Not everyone is your enemy, although sometimes it's hard to distinguish who is or is not in these troubled times. You must trust me if I am going to get you home. In the bag we brought you a little food and a change of clothes for your father. His garments are sure to bring attention to him. I will leave with Granny Smith and bring you breakfast and perhaps a change of clothes for you in the morning, but please don't complain they are not what you want; you have what you are given and they will be more suitable for travelling. While I am gone think on about your own appearance. Osbert is looking for a nobleman and his daughter, who is a young girl with long brown hair dressed like a young lady. Which is more important to you, your hair, your girly clothes, your lady like manner, or all our lives?"

"Tobias," Granny called from the shelter. "I am done here and will say my goodbyes."

"Coming Granny, I will walk with you apiece, wait for me," Toby answered as he came back to the shelter.

"Go inside and console your father. Stay out of sight, the light is fading and will soon be night. I will see you on the morrow early, but first if you will, pass me your father's blooded hose so that I can get rid of it," he asked Rebecca. Rebecca went into the shelter and passed out the hose. "Goodnight My Lord," he called to the nobleman.

"Goodnight and God speed." Sir Simon replied from inside the shelter.

"Where will you sleep tonight?" Rebecca asked.

"Don't concern yourself with that," he answered, "I will see you in the morning. You will both be safe here until I return."

Chapter Two

Toby left them both safe inside the shelter, and then he and Granny Smith walked across the clearing and headed back toward the village.

"I am going over to Ravenshead to see if I can steal food from the new priest's kitchen. No doubt Osbert will have installed his own man in that role now that he has murdered the one he couldn't corrupt. I will leave you at the edge of the village; if I hurry I should be back at the shelter by midnight. By stealing from the priest, I hope to set a false trail toward the hills to the west and Lord Chester's estate. It may give us breathing space. Will you be alright?" Toby asked Granny Smith. "I will come back to see you as soon as I can. Please be careful; don't give Osbert reason to suspect you of helping Sir Simon de Selis."

"Yes, I will be fine, but you watch yourself, there are soldiers searching everywhere, but then I suppose you know what you are doing. Watch the girl closely; she may unwittingly give you away. She has been brought up as a spoilt young lady and has to learn the ways of the world quickly. It will be hard for her, so be patient," advised Granny. They came up to the outskirts of the village. "Here's where you can leave me, I can make it from here, as your way lies elsewhere. Good Luck." With tears in her eyes, she reached out and gave Toby a hug. They held onto one another a while, then both turned and went their separate ways without a backward glance.

It took Toby half an hour to reach Ravenshead. It was almost dark now and he could see candle lights flickering in the houses, but there was no one on the streets. The Ale House at the end of the village, which doubled as a traveller's resting place, was also brightly lit much more than usual. Laughter, singing and raised voices told Toby that some of Osbert's men were in there; the villagers rarely used the place and travellers only to eat and sleep.

Staying in the shadows, Toby slowly made his way to the courtyard, which housed a small stable. There were two military horses tethered there, ready saddled, a wagon was stood in the far corner. But the horses which pulled it were inside the stables and not harnessed. There were no guards posted, so they were not expecting any trouble. Toby quickly moved toward the saddled horses and, using his skinning knife, cut the girth straps on both horses. When the chase was on they would be unable to take part, giving him a head start.

He left the courtyard and made his way to the rear of the building. A door opened and a woman came out carrying a bucket of scraps, which she emptied into one of the wooden bins standing just outside. He waited and watched as she lifted the hem of her apron to wipe the perspiration from her brow and then made her way back inside, leaving the door open. Moving closer, he could see that the open door led into the kitchen. On a table just inside he saw what was left of a leg of pork, enough to feed three people at least, and fresh bread. He moved closer still until he was at the door. This was too good an opportunity to miss; he could steal food from here instead of the priest's house and be away without being seen, then he could lay a trail for the soldiers to follow. He looked further inside; he could see no one in the kitchen at all, now was his chance. He went inside, and picking up an empty flour sack; he filled it with as much as he could comfortably carry on the run. He left quickly by the same door and ran out into the darkness of the night toward the road leading out of the village. Suddenly behind him there was a cry of,

"Stop thief! Stop. Help! There is a thief. Someone has stolen my meat. Help!" the woman cried.

"Drat! I thought I would have got clean away, or at least more of a head start," murmured Toby. "Ah well the chase is on now and I'm the quarry," Toby ran down the road heading west, trailing Sir Simon's blooded hose behind him, the hue and cry at his heels.

The night was clear and still with the sweet smell of wild dog roses drifting on a very slight breeze. The moon was nearly full and was lighting his way toward the forest. Behind him he could see men carrying burning torches and hear baying dogs that were following his scent, and then the shout of an angry Captain, who having lost his saddle was hating to be on foot, urging his drunken men on to catch this thief.

Toby knew this part of the country well. He led the chase into the forest and down toward the river. After ten minutes hard running he came upon a clearing, which he knew had a rabbit warren covering half of it, and headed straight for it. By this time Toby had left the drunken soldiers in his wake. Now was the time to get the dogs off his tail. He could tell by the amount of rabbit droppings and freshly dug soil that the warren was occupied. He stopped by a newly dug rabbit hole and, opening his sack, took out two fresh marrow bones, which he had taken from the kitchen. He took one of them and thrust it deep, arms length inside, and then moved a few yards away and put the other bone inside a different hole.

'Let's see what the dogs make of that,' he grinned. He found a patch of ground where the rabbit droppings were more numerous around a fresh dug hole. He hid some of the blooded hose inside it. He then ran from one rabbit hole to another all around the warren, dragging the rest of the blooded hose along the ground, and then placing the hose inside his coat, headed off toward the river.

A short time later the Captain and his men reached the clearing and the two dogs headed for the warren. When they found the hole where Toby had hidden the first bone, the dogs began furiously digging to get at it, but it was too far in for them to reach. One dog was pulled aside and told to find again the scent they had been following. The dog moved across the warren to the other hole where the second bone was buried and again started to frantically dig into the hole. The captain seeing this screamed at his dog handlers,

"What have you here, rabbit dogs? We are not here to catch rabbits, get them back on the trail or I will cut you up and feed you to your own useless animals."

The handlers pulled off the dogs and tried to find the trail once again but the dogs just run around from one hole to the other, continually coming back to where the bones were buried. After a while one of the handlers called out,

"They've lost the scent Captain; they're just running round in circles. They are trained to hunt animals not men."

"Get them out of my sight and you with them!" bellowed the Captain. "I will see you back at the barracks and you had better have a good reason for this you idiots. They should be able to hunt anything, including men." He was so angry he was blue in the face barking orders at his incompetent men. "Go back to the Ale House and find out when I will get my horse. It should not take all this time to repair or change a girth strap. Someone's head will roll for this and it's not going to be mine. You there, get the men together and move out at the double. I think he's heading for the river. If he reaches it he will be on Chester's land and we will lose him. Come on move yourself!" He screamed. The soldiers grudgingly moved out, secretly wishing that the quarry had crossed the river. After drinking all night, all they wanted was to get back to their beds.

Meanwhile Toby had reached the river. He knew they wouldn't follow onto Lord Chester's land without permission, as he had no liking for Baron Osbert either, but he was getting further away from where he had left Sir Simon and his daughter. It was time now to make his way back. Making sure he left footprints where he entered the water, he dropped what was left of Sir Simon's blooded hose on the ground, and crossed the river. Leaving more footprints on the far bank where he got out. He ran two hundred paces into the forest away from the river and into Lord Chester's land before stopping. Then, carefully covering his tracks as he went, walked in a large half circle ending up back at the river a good distance downstream. He then re-entered the water and continued to move downstream, moving north east to bypass Ravenshead and bring him closer to Glenford. He stayed in the cold water of the river a good distance, stopping only once at a deep point in the river to put his bag on the bank, take off his clothes, and bathe himself to wash the dirt and the smell of rabbit from him. Although he was cold and wet, it was a warm night, so he knew that he would quickly get warm again. He had not had a bath for quite some time and liked the feel of it. He dressed enough to be decent, picked up the rest of his clothes, his coat and bag, and then left the river and travelled quickly through the forest.

Meanwhile the soldiers had reached the river. The Captain ordered his men to search the river bank to determine where the fugitive had crossed. In their search they found the blooded garment Toby had planted there. They crossed the river and saw the footprints leading out into the forest onto Lord Chester's land. The Captain had no option but to call the chase off. Without orders he dare not pursue him over the river. He ordered his lieutenant to report at once to Baron Osbert in Nottingham, taking the blooded hose with him as proof it was Sir Simon de Selis whom they had chased over the river.

Glenford was quiet as Toby passed through on his way back to the shelter, just the odd light here and there flickering in the dwellings. Calm now, but Toby knew this village had known terror at the hands of Osbert in the past, as had all the villages in Osbert's control. As he made his way to the shelter; all he could hear now was the gentle rustle of leaves in the trees and the occasional call of a vixen to her cubs. The hounds and soldiers lost far behind him. He reached the shelter and silently crawled in without waking the sleeping fugitives. He lay down exhausted, his nights work done.

CHAPTER THREE

Dawn was breaking over the forest. All the forest birds were singing, joined as if in a choir, with the Song Thrush leading from the top of the tallest tree. A lark rose into the air joining this dawn chorus, singing his song as he ascended into the heavens greeting the new day.

Toby stirred and looked about him, he had heard natures symphonic ensemble many times before. In the gloom of the shelter he could see His Lordship and Rebecca already awake, watching him.

"Good morning My Lord, Rebecca," he greeted them, "I've brought you your breakfast, here help yourself," chucking the bag of food he had stolen toward them, "hope you like pork, I couldn't find venison," he grinned.

"Pork will do just fine, thank you. You must have gone to a lot of trouble to get this, we are very grateful," said his Lordship as they both tucked into the food Toby had provided. "I am known as Sir Simon de Selis but, while we are on the run, I think you should call me Simon in case we are overheard, don't you?" Inquired Sir Simon, "and my daughter can be called Becky, or Anne what do you think?"

"I like the name Anne." Toby replied. "If we are stopped by soldiers, we could be a family, with father Simon, his son Toby and daughter Anne, who were looking for work as farm workers until father had an accident with a scythe. Now we are heading home to Tickhill. "It will be hard to pull off, the locals know me, and if anyone looks at your hands, they will see you are not used to farm work." Then turning to Anne he said, "Cut me a piece of that pork please Anne, I need breakfast too."

"Yes, certainly I will. Just listen to the birds, don't they sound lovely," said Anne.

"Yes they do. It also means there is no one around or they would be silent. You must also learn to speak as farm folk do and drop any airs and graces as they stand out among ordinary folk. You don't say, 'yes certainly I will,' you just cut a piece and pass it over saying 'here y'are Toby.' It will be hard for you, believe me I know, but you must learn quickly if we are to survive: I will provide for you, although it will be meagre. I will try to keep you away from villages and people as much as I can, but we are bound to run into someone sometime. But that is for the morrow; today Simon, you must exercise that leg."

"Aye, that all sounds fine, I can't think of a better plan," Simon answered, "I am rather stiff, I do need to walk around to take the stiffness out of it,"

"I'll have a look round to make sure it's safe, and get you a staff to use as a crutch if you need it. I won't be long." With that he picked up a small axe that was in the corner of the shelter, placed it in his belt, crawled out and was gone.

"We must do as Toby asks. We don't know the area, the roads, or even the forest as Toby does, out there we are lost," Simon told Anne, "We must trust in him completely, put our lives in his hands. If it requires us to live like the lowest peasants, to live rough in the hedge-bottoms as we are now, and to eat what we are given, we must. Do you think you can do that?"

"Yes father, even though as you say, it means putting our lives in his hands," replied Anne, "I have a feeling he has done this kind of thing before, and he certainly knows his way around the forest, even at night, I did not hear him come into the shelter last night did you? And where do you suppose he obtained the food? If he had wanted to give us up he would have done so by now. Yes, I am willing to trust him."

At that moment Toby called to them from outside the shelter,

"You can come out, it's safe."

Simon and Anne crawled out of the shelter, with the help of Toby and his daughter, Simon struggled to get to his feet.

"It's good to be able to stand at last," said Simon, as he took the crutch that Toby had fashioned for him.

"How does the leg feel?" Anne enquired.

"Sore, very stiff and still rather painful, but better than yesterday at least I can stand," he tried to walk a few steps, "Ugh! It will be better when the stiffness goes I think, I will be fine afore long."

"Try walking a few paces into the forest and back. Go with him Anne and try not to leave any tracks. I'll go and catch our dinner." He went inside the shelter and retrieved his father's bow and arrows, then started to walk across the clearing. "I won't be long, and remember to keep quiet and out of sight, above all keep your eyes and ears open." He instructed, then with a wave he was gone into the forest.

Anne walked with her father a few steps at a time, stopping now and then to ease the pain, and then going on further into the forest. A few more steps each time, for about an hour, until they came to a fallen oak.

"Let us rest awhile before making our way back, we can sit on this oak and relax a short while." said Simon.

"I don't think I will ever relax again," answered Anne nervously looking round as they sat down.

"Just listen to the sounds of the forest," Simon urged, "you heard the birds this morning, even the trees talk if you listen to them. It can be very soothing, and listen, don't you hear the woodpecker?"

Anne listened, "Yes I hear it, but there's no one chasing him, he can afford to relax; I wonder how my new found brother is faring, don't you think we should be making our way back? It will be mid-morning when we arrive back at the shelter."

"You are beginning to like him now aren't you?" her father teased, "He has only been away a short time and you are missing him."

"Yes I am. But you had better not tell him that, do you hear? I do feel safe when he is around. He is so self assured. He has put his life in danger for our sake, and I know he will get us home, he is determined to do so," confessed Anne.

"Yes, I think he will," agreed her father as he rose up from his seat. "Have you fallen for this boy who lives in the hedge-rows? I'm sure you could get used to living like that if you tried."

"Oh father don't be silly, stop teasing me," she could feel the colour rise in her cheeks. "What if I have, he could learn to live in a grand house as we do, couldn't he?" Simon was walking better now, slowly and painfully, but with a limp, and leaning hard onto the crutch for help.

"He may not want to, and then what would you do? He hasn't the means to keep a wife in the fashion you are familiar with; he's just a poacher, a rabbit catcher. He would be put to death if he was caught."

"Enough! Please let the matter drop father; I could do anything if I put my mind to it, just let us get back to his shelter; but don't forget, rabbit catcher or poacher, it is his hands in which you have put our lives." Anne replied haughtily.

"Would you like me to break into a trot? I don't think I could at the moment," Simon smiled, "maybe tomorrow."

"Oh father, will you stop teasing. If you say anything of this to Toby, I shall never speak to you again."

They walked the rest of the way back without speaking, each deep in their own thoughts. They came upon the clearing close to the shelter. Simon stopped and looked around, as Toby would have done, seeing nothing untoward, they walked over to the stream and sat on the bank.

They had not sat there long when Toby arrived, taking three rabbits from under his coat, he grinned and threw them on the ground beside Anne.

"There you are Anne, skin those for us, any country girl would do that in a few minutes. I'll collect some firewood and then you can roast them for us. I think we can risk a fire there is no one around."

"Ugh! Its eyes are open, it's looking at me!" she squirmed, pulling a face and retching as if she was about to vomit, "please do not make me do that."

"I've cleaned the innards. The magpies have eaten those. You only have to take the skin, feet and head off and then roast them, it can't feel anything its dead," he laughed. Anne reached out and touched the one nearest to her. It was still warm; she shuddered and recoiled in horror. Simon couldn't help himself; he started to laugh uncontrollably, rolling over on the bank.

"What was that you were saying earlier?" he asked her. "I can do anything I put my mind to." he mimicked, and then went into another bout of laughter. Anne, afraid that her father would say more of their earlier conversation, screamed at him,

"Father don't you dare! Just don't you dare!" she got up and walked quickly back into the forest.

"What have I said?" Toby was puzzled by this outburst, "have I upset her?"

"No Toby, not you; Go after her and bring firewood on your way back. I will skin these. It's been a long time, but I haven't forgotten how." Simon answered. "Be gentle with her she is a sensitive soul and is trying hard to come to terms with our circumstances." Tony followed and quickly caught up with Anne.

"I suppose you have come to gloat," she snapped.

"Gloat, why?" he asked, "I don't wish to see you upset, I was only teasing about the rabbits."

"It wasn't you, and it was nothing to do with the wretched rabbits. It was father and his constant teasing," Anne thought for a moment . . . "Alright I will tell you," she continued, "I told Father earlier that you had been gone a long time and that I was missing you, that I had feelings for you, and feel safe when you are around. He said I couldn't live the way you do, but I said I could, and that I could do anything I put my mind to. So when you brought the rabbit for me to skin and I could not, he laughed and made fun of me. There, now you know. Now you too can have a good laugh at my expense." Toby took hold of her shoulders and gently drew her toward him,

"Do you really have feelings for me?" he asked.

Anne looked into his eyes,

"Yes I do," she replied, "but there's no point to it. We are worlds apart in station, I could not live like you, nor you like me, so there's an end to it."

"I have feelings for you too." Toby declared. "Will you wait until all this is over before you put an end to it?" Toby asked, "Then you will see, things are not always as they seem. But please, don't ask me more until then."

Anne looked hard into Toby's eyes, as if looking for more answers, seeing the sincerity in his face she said,

"Yes, I will wait until this nightmare is over Toby, although I cannot see how things would change for us to be together, but . . . I think you do, so yes I will wait and see how you think you can change things, Thank you Toby."

"Then let us collect firewood before your father eats the rabbits raw."

That remark brought the smile back to Anne's face. He showed her how to pick the dead, dry wood, which would not smoke too much when they made the fire. With an armful each they made their way back to the stream. Simon looked curiously at the glow and the smile on Anne's face when she returned, but dare not ask why. Toby just went to work quietly as he always did and very soon the fire was burning well. He cut three thick willow wands that grew by the stream and showed Anne how to insert them into the rabbits as a skewer, and then place them over the fire to roast on others he had already stuck into the ground each side of the fire. Simon was amazed that she could now touch the raw animals without being squeamish.

"What have you said to her?" Simon asked Toby, "Whatever it is, I like it."

"Be quiet father," said Anne.

"Yes, shut up father," said Toby as he turned the rabbits on the spit. Now it was Anne's turn to laugh.

"And you Anne, I will teach you how to catch, kill, skin and roast a rabbit before our journey's over. They are not normally meat for Lords and Ladies nowadays, although your ancestors brought them to England to breed as meat for the table. Some escaped and are now wild but, they will keep us alive."

Anne stopped laughing. While she watched him turning the food on the skewers, her thoughts turned to what he had said to her earlier in the forest. What did he mean when he said things are not what they seem? And why could he not tell her more? After a while she suddenly realized he had just said she would learn to kill and skin rabbits, this brought her back down to earth. Kill rabbits! She couldn't do that.

"Is there nothing else to eat in the forest but rabbit?" she asked.

"Aye," answered Toby as he tried the roast, "we may catch pigeon, partridge or pheasant, and there are always nuts and berries at this time of year," he took the roast from the fire, "these are ready to eat but mind you don't burn your fingers. Hold the ends of the skewer as I do," he demonstrated, then continued. "There are ducks and geese, also fish in the rivers we will be crossing as we travel north, all to be skinned or plucked, and then gutted before roasting. That's if it's safe to light a fire, if not we eat it raw." Then seeing the look of repulsion on Anne's face said, "Don't worry, it's not as bad as it sounds. But if we are caught stealing his Lordship's game, we could get a public whipping or have an eye taken out, or even a hand chopped off to serve as a warning to others who would steal from him." He handed a rabbit from the fire over to Simon. "I know your father has eaten rabbit afore, how do you like it Anne?"

"Yes, it was rather nice until you told me that," she answered, "I'm rather surprised; it's not nearly as bad as I thought it was going to be. I think I prefer this to fowl."

"Good, because you will eat a lot of them before we get o'er the Don. No one minds me taking a few rabbits, they eat the crops. But they don't like me taking game birds, boar or deer. They are wanted for his Lordship's hunting parties, 'though he's not been hunting for a while. We have bread and cheese for supper and there's a little pork left. We will eat what we catch when that's gone." Toby told them. "I am going to scout ahead later, just to make sure there are no surprises waiting for us. We can relax until then."

"You serve us well Toby. We will never be able to repay you in full. Take care and don't put your life in danger for our sake," said Simon, "Thomas did that and paid with his life. I don't want your life on my conscience also."

"I've already done that by bringing you here, but don't worry, I'm not ready to die just yet, I have plans for my future," Toby answered. "Are you ready to receive a visitor?"

"A visitor, where, who?" asked a startled Anne jumping to her feet, "I don't see anyone."

"Listen, the forest is telling you. The birds have stopped singing, all is quiet . . . And I have just spied Granny Smith across the clearing." grinned Toby.

"You have sharp ears and eyes," Simon observed, "I don't see anyone."

"Then its good it is not Osbert's men," said Toby. "Granny Smith did say she would come to fix your dressing today." He stood and beckoned Granny to come forward.

"Good day to you all, my but that rabbit smells good," she greeted them, "don't suppose there's any left?"

"Here have half of mine Granny," offered Anne, "I can't eat a whole one."

Granny sat on the bank. "Why thank you Miss Rebecca, we can't waste good food can we. I've brought you a loaf and cheese to take on your journey." She took the piece of rabbit and started to eat. "And how is the leg My Lord, feeling better I hope?"

"Much better thanks to your healing powers, and Toby's care. But there are no lords and ladies here. For the time being I am Simon of Tickhill, and this is my daughter Anne."

"I thought your leg was fully healed! You must be eating well too, I'm told you stole half a pig, butter, cheese and bread from the Ale House at Ravenshead. Then ran away onto Lord Chester's land, where the soldiers could not follow and now I see you eating rabbit, and very good tasting rabbit too. Now how did you do all that with that ailing leg of yours I wonder?" Said Granny sarcastically, and then turning to Toby she said, "Osbert has put most of his men on Chester's border after he found Sir Simon's blooded hose by the river. He is demanding Lord Chester finds his Lordship and hand him over within one week, or he threatens to cross the river in force to find him."

"So that is where you went last night," interrupted Simon, "laying a false trail onto the Earl of Chester's land, and a good one by the sound of it. I am amazed at your strategic resourcefulness. Ranulf is quite strong enough to see Baron Osbert off. When we get home I will see that Osbert knows of it, and then he will leave the Earl be. But you do take risks Toby."

"That risk has bought us time," said Toby. "We leave on the morrow at daybreak and hope to have you o'er the River Don in three to four days, for now let Granny tend your leg."

"I have fresh clothing for Anne as you asked for, and a couple of farmers smocks for them to wear, so that they at least look like farm labourers. Take Anne to where the stream bends, the water is deeper there, she can bathe and change into garments more fitting a farm girl. Cut off that hair too to prevent fleas. Farm girls don't usually have long hair for that reason. It will draw attention to her."

"Come Anne," Toby offered his hand, "I'll show you the place."

Anne picked up the garments, took Toby's hand and walked along the clearing following the stream. When they arrived at the bend Toby took out his knife.

"Do you want me to cut your hair first, before I leave you to bathe? I will stay in earshot, so call if you want me."

"Yes, cut it if you must, though under protest. I shall look horrible. How much will you take?"

"I will cut it very short, but don't worry it will grow again." he grinned

Toby went to work cutting her hair; Anne winced with every cut, until it was all done. He picked up the hair that was lying on the ground,

"We can't leave this for someone to find, so while you bathe I will take it away and burn it."

"Oh my lovely hair, what have I done!" Anne said with tears rolling down her cheeks. "No you shall not burn it; I will make a keepsake with it, please! I will be careful, please?" she begged taking it from him.

"Alright, but keep it hidden or it will give the game away," he warned, "Now get rid of those fancy clothes and go take your bath, or do you want me to help with that too?" Toby walked menacingly toward her.

"Toby, you wouldn't . . . you wouldn't . . . No you wouldn't," she said as Toby walked toward her. She backed away holding him at arm's length "No Toby you wouldn't Eeeek!" Anne fell backward into the stream. Splash, "Ugh! Toby you, you! Ooh! It's cold!"

Toby laughed out loud,

"Then get bathed quickly, or shall I come and bathe you?" Toby made a move toward her.

"You wouldn't dare," Toby took a further step, "No, no, no thank you. I can manage. Toby-e-e! I can manage, go away, Toby-e-e-e!" she moved back, away from his advances, her thoughts telling her, yes this young man would dare anything, that is why she is drawn to him.

"Alright, but don't be long, I'll just take a look around. Wait here I'll be back shortly."

Toby turned and moved silently into the forest. Anne undressed and, fearing Toby would return and find her naked, bathed and dressed quickly, putting on the clothes that Granny had brought for her. She then wrung all the water she could out of her old wet garments and hung them onto a hawthorn bush to dry. When Toby returned she was sat on the bank waiting for him. He sat by her side asking,

"Have you seen a scruffy looking female with a lot of airs and graces here? I told her to wait for me, but disobedient as ever she must have wandered off somewhere. I shall have to put a stick to her backside, to teach her to do as she's told."

Anne jumped up and threw herself on top of him. Toby fell onto his back. Anne's knees were astride him, her fists flailing at his chest.

"Put a stick to me would you? Scruffy looking am I?" she cried continuing to pummel him. "Disobedient am I? Teach me to do as I'm told will you?"

Toby started to laugh out loud.

"Don't you dare laugh at me you monster; I will teach you some manners, I will teach you how to treat a lady." Toby grabbed her arms and rolled her over, now he was astride her, pinning her down.

"I see no ladies here on which to use good manners, only a common farm girl, good looking, but one I would readily put a stick to if she doesn't do as she's told." Toby laughed. Anne stopped struggling, she looked up at Toby. Was this the young man who only yesterday she could not trust? Who was this young man who was risking his life for her and her father? And who in the space of one day she could develop such feelings toward, enough to trust him with their lives? He had come to their aid giving them shelter, providing them with food, and had even found a healer for her father who they could also trust, without being asked. She had questions to ask of him, but had promised not to. He had never mentioned his parents. He acted and lived like a common peasant, catching rabbits to make his way, but Anne could see that he had the bearing, education and intelligence of someone of higher station. In his company Anne was relaxed and felt safe.

"Oh Toby!" she whispered, "I wish this day would never end. I'm so happy here in the forest with you; no fighting, no killing, just peace and quiet."

Toby let her up and sat on the bank of the stream beside her, his face had lost the smile; he was looking more serious now.

"That would soon end if Osbert were to find us; until he and others like him are brought to justice there will always be fighting and killing. I wait for that day. It is the lust for power that drives men like him. The more they have the more they want. I wait for the day when they are no more and all England is free."

He saw that Anne was looking at him differently now. She had never seen him in this mood before, all solemn and serious. She was seeing a man emerging from this youth, but before she could utter the questions that were on her lips he rose to his feet.

"Come, we must get back your father will be waiting, you need to show him your new clothes." Picking up her old clothes, Anne followed obediently without saying a word.

When they arrived back at the shelter Simon and Granny Smith were sat by the fire chatting. Anne stood in front of her father.

"Do you like your new clean daughter?" she asked.

"Yes I do," Simon answered. "I like your hair too, but I would have cut it shorter I think."

"Then you would have me bald like an old man, as you will be one day," she grinned. "These clothes are a very rough material, they irritate my skin," she complained. "I know," she said putting her hand up to stop any comment, "I have to get used to them, and I will, but I may have scratched all the skin from my body first. But I am grateful for what you have done for us Granny Smith. Thank you."

"Come, let us go a short walk to stretch my stiff joints," said Simon, "Granny can tell Toby all the local news."

Anne helped him to his feet and they both set off into the forest toward the fallen oak. Granny let them get out of earshot.

"I have eyes in my head, and they tell me that you and that young lady are becoming very close. Please be careful Tobias, I don't want you to get hurt. His Lordship was asking lots of questions regarding Osbert; I answered them as truthfully as I could without telling him anything personal. He asked if I would be witness to his brutality if it was brought to the King's notice. I told him I thought the King was more interested in keeping his throne, than his subjects' welfare. He takes the word of his cousin Maud before all others, yet she is the one trying to steal his crown."

"Don't worry, yes I have feelings for Anne as she has for me, but that is how it will stay. I mean to get them safe, and then ask for their help to clear my family name, but they don't know it yet." Toby answered, "I have plans for my future as I told you afore, and you are in them too. We shall both sleep sound in our beds when this is ended. I need allies that I can trust, strong allies like Sir Simon de Selis and his friend the Archbishop of York. If I show my trustworthiness and honesty, I may get them to speak to the King on my behalf."

"You are playing a dangerous game Tobias. Knight will not speak against knight for fear it rebounds on them. Cousins and even brothers have been put to the sword on false charges of treason, as you well know, but I can understand why you are doing this, and when the time comes I will be here for you. God bless and keep you safe," said Granny. She got to her feet, "I will go home now and wait your safe return."

"Thank you for your help, and your support. There is a pheasant and a rabbit hanging in the fork of the dead birch as you cross the stream. I'm sure you can make use of them. I caught them while Anne was bathing." He took Granny in his arms and held her close.

"That's enough of that, I must get home. I need to pick a few herbs on the way, some for healing and some for the bird I mean to enjoy for lunch tomorrow. Thank you, Tobias. If you can get salt from somewhere, then put a handful in boiling water and clean the wound with it tomorrow evening, which should suffice until he meets his own healer.

She left with a wave of her hand, crossed the clearing and disappeared into the forest. Toby stood and watched until she was out of sight. He then went into the shelter, cut himself a piece of bread and chunk of cheese, put them inside his coat, picked up his bow and arrows and then followed Simon and Anne into the forest.

He came upon them as they were sat resting on the fallen oak, they had not seen him. He circled around behind them like an animal stalking its prey, keeping out of sight, yet silently getting closer until he was no more than five paces from them. He could overhear their conversation. It was more or less repeating what Granny had told him, but with Simon adding that he would ask the Archbishop to help him bring Osbert and his fellow conspirators to book for treason in the King's name. That was what Toby was longing to hear. He came out of the bushes and stood upright behind them. The pair being engrossed in such deep conversation, still they failed to hear him. He touched Simon on the shoulder. Startled, he jumped to his feet drawing a dagger as he did so, turning to face whoever it was behind him. Anne too jumped to her feet and took refuge behind her father.

"If I had been one of Osbert's men, you would have been dead before you knew they were there. I keep telling you to keep your eyes and ears sharp." Toby told them forcefully. "I can't be with you all the time."

"Point taken and lesson learned." Simon said sheathing his dagger.

"You scared me out of my wits," said Anne.

"Better be scared than dead Anne, and the lesson is only learned if it doesn't happen again Simon. How can a knight of the realm get caught out so easily? You must be on your guard at all times, next time you may be dead. Osbert's men don't stop to pass the time of day. Do you understand?"

"As a knight I was taught to fight honourably, in open battle, army on army, knight on knight, but I will heed of your words, it will not happen again."

"You have a pretty little farm girl to look after. I would love to do it for you, but I don't mix with farm girls" Toby grinned. Anne slapped his arm. "You know what would happen to your daughter if Osbert's soldiers caught you. I have to go on a few miles, to find the safest way for us to travel come daybreak. Osbert will not have sent all his men to Chester's border, he is too clever for that, he has learned to fight in a different way, without honour," Toby made to leave. "Go back to the shelter; keep your eyes and ears open. I hope to be back by nightfall if not I will see you at daybreak. Get a good night's sleep we have far to go."

"Take care Toby and come back to us," said Anne, "You may not mix with farm girls, but we will always have a place for you."

"That is the truth of it," said Simon. Toby set off into the forest travelling north toward Stowe.

Simon and Anne set off back to the shelter. Simon chastising himself for allowing Toby to get the better of him that way,

"I must learn from him, and learn quickly if I am to get us home safely. I must learn to live like a hunted animal by instinct, as Toby does. He was right; I should never have allowed anyone to get that close to me without my knowing, especially as I have to protect you also."

"Do not torture yourself so father you will learn from Toby, he will be a good tutor I think. How is your leg? Do you think you can walk far on it?" asked Anne.

"Not as far or as fast as I would like," replied Simon. "It is still stiff and quite painful but I will be alright as long as I don't have to run."

They came to the clearing. Simon stopped and looked around. Seeing nothing out of place they both walked over toward the shelter, Simon rekindled the dying embers of the fire, and sat on the bank beside the stream.

"There is bread, butter and cheese in the shelter that Granny brought us. Shall I get it father?" asked Anne. "It will be our last meal today."

"No," he answered, "save it for an early supper. I will just sit and rest my leg. I have a lot of thinking to do so I will sit here quietly listening to the birds." Anne did not answer, she went into the shelter and brought out a small bag she had fashioned from a piece of her old dress, opened it and took out the shorn locks of her hair which she had saved and began to plait them into a long strand. They both sat on the bank not speaking until the light began to fade,

Simon broke the silence, "Shall we have a bite to eat now, the fire is burnt low and it's getting chilly? We can then retire early."

"As you wish father," Anne replied. She put her hair back into the bag, returned it to the shelter, and brought out the food. "Have you done with your thinking father?" she asked.

"For now," he cut himself a piece of bread. "Don't you worry your head about such matters; it will all be fine when we get home."

They sat awhile eating their meal by the dying embers of the fire. When they had finished Anne's thoughts turned to Toby.

"I wonder what Toby is doing; I do hope he is alright he's been gone for hours. I thought he would have been back by now."

"He will be fine, that young man can take care of himself." Simon assured her. "The days almost gone, come let's away to our beds such as they are."

They both entered the dark shelter and began to settle down for the night. Simon continued,

"Toby was right about this place. Granny Smith did say the soldiers had searched the village. We would have been caught had we asked for shelter there, yet no one would think of looking for us here. When it comes to knowing the ways of a fugitive, he is the master. I wonder how long he has been that way, but more to the point, why?"

"I don't know. He will tell us in his own good time I think. Goodnight father."

"Goodnight Anne, We start our journey home at daybreak, so sleep well."

"Goodnight to both of you," a voice spoke from the other end of the shelter. Both Simon and Anne jumped to a sitting position.

"What! How did you get in here without our hearing you?" asked a startled Anne.

"I could have brought an army in with me. You talk so much you hear nothing but your own voices. 'Point taken lesson learned," he mimicked, "I think you will never learn. I'm tired and need to sleep, Goodnight, sleep well."

Toby lay down to sleep at their feet. Not wanting to disturb him more and feeling rather embarrassed at being caught and chastised a second time, Simon and Anne lay down to sleep with just a "Goodnight Toby."

CHAPTER FOUR

WHEN DAWN BROKE the next morning, Simon woke and looked around him, through the gloom he could see that Toby had already left the shelter. He shook Anne.

"Anne, wake up. Toby's already up and about, come on sleepyhead we have to leave." Anne sat up.

"Go on father. I will collect my things and follow."

Simon went outside to find Toby had already made a fire and was roasting a pheasant and a couple of rabbits.

"Morning Simon," he greeted him.

"Good morning Toby. Looks like you've been up some time."

"Yes, I lit the fire and put the food to roast, it's about ready. I caught and dressed them on my way back last night. We can leave when we've had our meal."

"About last night Toby, I'm sorry I didn't hear you come back into the shelter, it's just that when we are in there it feels safe." Simon explained.

"In these times you are not safe in your own home," said Toby.

Anne joined them by the fire.

"From this point on we shall all have to be more vigilant and guarded in what we say and how we say it. When we leave here we become hunted animals if we wish to stay alive . . . Eat your food." He took the food from the fire and laid it on a bed of large comfrey leaves. Cutting a breast from the pheasant he handed it to Anne. "Try this, see if you like it, if not there is rabbit."

"Thank you, and good morning," said Anne.

Toby continued, "We must take what is left with us, but only carry what a farm worker would, food and clothing nothing more. I'm afraid you will have to leave your sword behind and any other trappings that would identify you Simon."

"I will be loath to do so, that sword was my father's." Simon replied. "But I understand."

"Wrap it inside Anne's old dress, leave it at the back of the shelter covered in the bracken we used for bedding, it will still be there when you return to oust Osbert." said Toby. "How do you like the pheasant Anne? Help yourself to more if you need it, we shall not eat again 'til noon."

"Thank you, I've eaten my fill." Anne replied.

"Then take what's left of the meat and wrap it in this rabbit skin," he said tossing a skin toward her, "I'll do the same with the rabbit then put the bones onto the fire." He then split the stalk of a mature bracken leaf to make a tie, tied the two bundles like two pouches and put them in the flour sack. Anne watched in silent amazement at the ease with which he did that. "Were you taught to fight with a staff when becoming a knight?" he asked Simon tossing him a long stout staff. "It's not a sword, but in the right hands I've seen it to be every bit as good. And it will serve as a crutch too."

"You dumfound me Toby; yes I am skilled with a staff, I won't feel naked with this in my hand."

"Then we are ready, we go by the way of Stowe and hope to dine by the Meden come midday if all goes to plan." Toby picked up his bow and led the way.

After they had been walking for an hour Toby stopped for them to rest, and for him to explain what was in front of them.

"Our first danger will be when we cross the Newark road. Baron Osbert's men guard that road to prevent outlaws robbing the traders and merchants who travel on it. He then charges them taxes for the protection. Osbert will have told them to watch for you. So it will be better not to be seen at all. They will question everyone."

"We are in your hands Toby and will do as you say," said Simon, "but one thing I would ask, if we do run into trouble I want you to get Anne to safety and take her to my friend the Archbishop in York."

"No!" cried Anne, "I shall not leave you; we must all go to York or none."

"Have I your word Toby?" Simon asked.

"No, father No!" Anne protested.

"I will promise to protect her with my life," answered Toby, "providing that I am allowed to take a stick to her if she is disobedient."

"Then I agree." Simon laughed.

"Why you, the pair of you have no right to . . ."

"Be quiet. Children should be seen but not heard," said Simon.

"That's quite right." Toby laughingly agreed.

"Children, how dare you,—ugh! Lots of children my age are already married and have children of their own," Anne retorted, "and you are not much older than me Toby!"

"We are all talking too much. The Newark road is just through that stand of trees, keep quiet and stay close. When we get to the trees I will go in front to see if the way is clear, when I beckon, come quickly. Remember be silent, don't even whisper, sound travels a long way in the forest." Toby reminded them.

They moved forward into the trees. As they came close to the road Toby gestured they stay still, while he moved forward to the road. He waited looking and listening for a few minutes and, when he thought it was safe, beckoned them to come forward. They hurried across the road together, and went into the forest on the far side. With Toby leading the way, they moved well away from the road and came upon a small stream before he spoke.

"We can rest awhile if you wish. We are still a few miles from Stowe; it's a mixture of farmland and forest hereabout. We will get back into the thick forest again when we reach the Ollerton road. That will be our next danger point. How is the leg holding up?"

"It is uncomfortable. Yes, I do need to rest it awhile," Simon answered. "I know I am slowing us down. This wretched leg of mine won't go as well as it should, sorry Toby!"

"We are not doing too badly, we have covered half the distance I set for today." Toby assured him. "I will go on and see how the land lies. Try to keep out of sight and keep your voices down. It will be easier walking on farmland for a time, but there is less cover, which means we have to be more alert. You have food in your bag Anne; eat the rest of the pork between you while you are resting. You don't want to be caught carrying that do you? It will give the game away if we are searched. I will take some meat from the last meal with me. I won't be long."

Toby left. Simon and Anne sat leaning against a weeping willow by the stream. After they had finished the pork and some of the bread, Anne removed her footwear and put her feet into the cool water to soothe them.

"Are they very sore?" asked her father.

"A little, I'm not used to walking over fields and through forests, but I shall be alright," Anne answered.

They both sat listening to the sounds around them. Sounds Anne hadn't noticed before came flooding to her ears; the trees rustling in the wind, birds singing in the tree tops, a pheasant calling in the distance, the water tumbling over stones in the stream. All this was new to her, but at the same time very calming and peaceful. Just for a short time she could feel relaxed and safe while she waited for Toby to return. She opened her small bag and took out the hair she had been plaiting and continued with it. They sat there without speaking for some time, when Anne noticed that the birds had suddenly gone quiet.

"Listen father," she whispered.

"What is it?" he asked.

"All is quiet, the birds, they have stopped singing." Then remembering what Toby had said, "Someone must be nearby."

"Keep your head down while I take a look," Simon told her as he turned to look around. "It's Toby, he's back." Seeing no one else, they both sat up. Toby sat beside them.

"Glad to see you on your toes. Are you rested and ready to move on?" he asked.

"Yes we are ready," Simon replied. "What have you found out?"

"Good and bad news. You have a price on your head, of five gold coins. Every cut throat and outlaw around will be looking to cash in on you." Toby told him. "And there is a score of Osbert's men patrolling all five roads out of Ollerton. So from now on we keep away from anyone we see."

"And what is the good news?" Simon asked.

"Your Archbishop has heard of your plight. He has left York with a hundred men at arms. He approaches Doncaster to be joined by Sir William Peveril, who has the finest archers in England under his command. Together they will then march south toward Tickhill."

"Where did you get this information, and how true is it?" he asked Toby.

"They are looking for a knight and his daughter, not a rabbit catcher. As such I can go where you cannot. I went into the market place at Stowe and overheard a soldier telling his wife, and that she should keep off the streets. He also said that if the Archbishop came in the King's name, the soldiers would not fight him but join him against Osbert. I believe that. They are all Englishmen forced into serving Osbert and have felt his boot." Toby continued. "We must cross the Meden today and rest on Lord Pierreport's land for the night. I have a small shelter there. My Lord Pierreport is away at court with King Stephen at the moment, leaving his daughter Lady Monica in charge of his estate. She is loyal to King Stephen and is good to her workers. They in turn are loyal to her. We can then with good fortune, meet up with your friend the Archbishop tomorrow at Tickhill."

"I have met Lady Monica," said Simon. "So devoted to her widowed father she never married. Doesn't she have a priory on her land that she makes donations to? I have heard of her generosity with the poor and destitute."

"Yes, the prioress there is also known for helping the poor with food from her gardens but we cannot trust her," Toby answered, "we can trust no one, not even Lady Monica herself for fear of one word spoken out of place. Come now we must get on."

Toby set off along the hedgerow. Anne and Simon walked behind in single file. They made good progress through the fields, passing east of Clipstone village and entered the forest again west of Stowe where they crossed the river Maun. As they were skirting Stowe village, they came to the road leading west from Ollerton. Toby went forward as before, Anne and Simon waiting in the trees. They saw him dive low behind bushes at the roadside. Moments later they heard horses' hooves and men talking and laughing. They waited, crouched down behind a large oak, holding their breath and not daring to move. The men and horses passed by. Toby waited a short time for them to get out of eyesight and then once more looked up and down the road. When he saw all was clear he beckoned them to come forward. They crossed the road without speaking and went deep into the forest. When they reached a small glade, Toby stopped and turned to them both.

"They were Osbert's men, I recognized their livery," he said. "They were heading toward Stowe. We have one more road ahead to cross at Budby, to reach Lord Pierreport's land, and cross the river Meden. We can stay there as I had planned or, if you are fit enough to go further, we can reach the river Poulter, leaving only a few miles to travel on the morrow."

"How many are a few?" asked Anne.

"I'm not sure, ten or twelve." Toby answered, "Are your feet too sore to go on? We can stay in the shelter by the Meden tonight, and then split the journey tomorrow. It would mean two more nights in the dirty hedgerows for you, can you put up with that?"

"Now you are mocking me! Yes I can!" Anne exclaimed irritably. "I was thinking more of father. He is struggling to keep up and needs to rest, and yes my feet are sore but I shall not complain. I am grateful for what you are doing."

"I'm sorry Anne that was wrong of me," said Toby, "you have put up with a lot these last few days that no lady should, and kept your spirits high, I admire you for that, forgive me." Turning to Simon Toby asked, "How is the leg? We can rest here awhile if you wish."

"Just a short time I have no wish to prolong our journey, but I am in some pain," answered Simon.

"Then rest awhile, I will go on to Budby and check the road. There is a fletcher there who will trade with me. I need a few more arrows and a couple of old bow strings to use as snares. I have a few coins. He knows my trade; his wife likes a rabbit now and then."

"Toby, wait a minute," Anne called as he turned to leave; she fumbled in her bag and brought out a necklet she had woven from the locks of her hair. "Wear this for me, it will be a lucky charm to keep you safe." She hung it round his neck, it had a rabbits foot fastened to it which was hanging onto his chest. "I have one too, just the same." Toby just smiled, and then left.

Anne watched him go, so pleased that he had accepted it. She then settled down beside her father to wait for his return. Toby returned a short time later, his quiver full of arrows and a smile on his face.

"The patrols are not as frequent on this road, there is talk of you being caught on Chester's land and Osbert is trying to negotiate to have you returned to him. For the time being, there is no one here looking for you. The fletcher's wife gave me a turnip and some beans from her garden to make a stew, and a loaf of bread in exchange for a couple of rabbits that I promised to take for her tonight. I have also some salt to clean your wound, and clean cloth to dress it. Anne or I can do that for you when we get to my other shelter, it's not too far."

"I knew that charm would bring you luck," said Anne gleefully.

"Spreading word that they are no longer looking for you could also be an Osbert trick to get us to drop our guard," Toby told her, "How are you Simon? Can you walk another couple of miles? I have been to my shelter and put in fresh bedding. No one has been around since I was last there some months ago. We can build a fire and rest for the night."

"You amaze me Toby. You travel around as fast and as quiet as the rabbits you hunt, you know the area and people in it like the back of your hand, and you have the senses of sight, hearing and smell better than most animals I know. We are very fortunate that you found us as you did; otherwise I dread to think where we would be now, or what our fate would have been. How can I ever repay you Toby? And in answer to your question, yes we can move on now, I am well rested."

Toby helped Simon to stand, "When we meet your friends, I will tell you how you can repay me, until then let us concentrate on getting you both safely to them."

They started out once again. Toby saw Simon was leaning more on his staff than before, so he decided to slow the pace even more to allow him to keep up. It wasn't long before they came upon the road leading to the northwest from Ollerton. Toby once again making sure the road was clear before they crossed onto Lord Pierreport's land on the other side, where he picked up the bag of turnip and bread he had obtained from the fletchers wife and hidden there earlier. Shortly after they reached and crossed the River Meden, they came to another of Toby's shelters at the side of a clearing, well hidden under a clump of Hawthorne bushes, again with a small stream nearby.

"It's well past midday. We have travelled a few miles today so we shall stay here tonight. I will gather wood and make a fire," said Toby, "why don't you soak your feet in the stream Anne, and when the fire is lit, you can get a pot from inside the shelter and cut up the beans and turnip ready to cook it,"

"I can't wait to get my feet into that water," said Anne, "are you sure you don't want me to collect the firewood first, I will?"

"Alright, you know how; your father can light the fire when you are ready.

I will go and find something to put in the pot with the turnip." Toby picked up his bow and arrows and moved across the clearing.

Anne gathered wood for the fire from the edge of the forest, being careful to collect only the dry wood the way Toby had shown her previously, and then returned to the shelter where her father was waiting to light the fire. Anne went into the shelter to bring out the pot to boil the stew. It was a much smaller place than the last one, but for one night she thought it would be big enough. There were two iron pots and some other earthenware bowls in a corner, just inside the entrance. She selected an iron pot with a handle, which she thought looked similar to the cooking pots she had seen in the kitchens at home, along with three of the bowls. When she came out, she picked up the bag containing the turnips and beans and then went to the stream to dangle her feet in the water. While at the same time, using her father's dagger and with some difficulty, because daggers were not meant to be used as kitchen knives, she sat preparing the vegetables for the meal. The fire was going well and the vegetables were prepared when Toby returned,

"How does stewed pheasant appeal to you?" he asked the waiting pair, handing Anne two ready prepared birds for the pot. "I'll get you the irons to hold the pot from the shelter"

"Thank you Toby, they will be fine," said Anne. "Now come and rest until it is ready to eat, you deserve it."

Simon watched his daughter as she cooked the meal. He was seeing the complaining young girl of a couple of days ago, change into a capable young woman, doing things he would never have dreamt she could do, living the life of a peasant girl and not complaining. He was so proud of her.

The meal was enjoyed by everyone, and there was plenty left for an evening meal. They could relax now for a short time. Anne could rest her sore feet and Simon could have his injured leg cleaned and re-dressed. Toby looked around him, pleased with the way their journey had progressed in the circumstances, and how he had managed until now to keep them from being seen by anyone.

"What is the plan now Toby?" Simon enquired.

"We should follow the north road, keeping to the forest where we can for cover," Toby answered. "We should pass to the east of the market town of Worksop, and on perhaps as far as Langold, which is a little further north, depending how your leg holds up. We will have to find shelter, or perhaps make a shelter there. I don't know the area north of Worksop well, so it will be a matter of checking as we go. Perhaps it would be better to stay overnight near Carlton village, just the other side of Worksop, and then it's not too far to Tickhill the day after. That should mean we will arrive there at the same time as your brother."

"I don't know this area either," said Simon, "but get me north to Tickhill, and we shall have friends to help. Sir Roger de Busli has men at arms; he lives there and is a good friend from the last crusade. I have a home on the River Dearne at Adwick, less than a score of miles on from there. I can send word to my men; they would meet us at Tickhill. Then we will be safe."

"Until then you are still Simon, and we still have two days travel to get out of Osbert's reach." Toby replied, then turning to Anne asked. "Do you think you could get the other cooking pot from the shelter, half fill it with water and put it on the fire to boil? When it is boiling, put in some of the salt from the bag, then let it cool enough not to scold you. While it is cooling take the old dressing from your father's leg and then bathe the wound with the salt water. When that is done, use the clean cloth to re-dress the wound. If you feel you cannot, I will do it when I return."

"I don't think I can do that Toby. I can boil the water, but I don't think I can touch the wound." Anne answered.

"Then fetch the pot and I will do it now, and you can help me, then you will know how," said Toby. "Afterward I have a promise to keep. I must pay for the food and the arrows; and need to catch rabbits to do so. If you keep the fire going, we can roast a couple to take with us tomorrow."

"I will do that to keep the stew warm for your return." Anne replied, and then asked, "How do you know you will catch so many rabbits?" Toby just smiled.

"Perhaps I will show you one day," he said.

The water was boiling. Simon removed his hose and lay on the ground, with just his shirt to cover his modesty. Toby took his skinning knife and cut away the bandages.

"The poultice Granny put on has done its work. Look Anne how clean the wound is." Anne looked at the wound and then turned away.

"Watch what I do Anne, one day you may be required to do this when there is no one else." Anne came back to watch as Toby bathed the wound. "There you see, nothing to it, just make sure everything is clean. Here you continue while I cut the cloth into strips."

Anne took the cloth and continued to bathe the wound, looking occasionally at her father's face, to see if there was any hurt in it. Although the salt was stinging the wound, Simon was astounded to see his daughter do this kind of thing and hid the pain. Toby handed her a piece of cloth to cover the wound and then the strips of cloth to bind it. When it was finished, Simon took her hand and said,

"Well done my daughter, I am proud of you."

"I knew you could do it," Toby told her, "you see, you can do anything you put your mind to. Now why don't you use the rest of the salt water to bathe those blisters on your feet?" Anne was pleased they were both proud of her. She took a piece of cloth and began to bathe the blisters on her feet, while Simon dressed.

"Eeeek!" she howled, "did it sting your wound like that?" Both Simon and Toby were laughing too much to answer. "You devils, you knew it would sting," then burst out laughing herself. "I will remember this and pay you back one day."

"It will do them good. Keep the pot warm I won't be long."

Toby picked up his bow and arrows and left to fulfil his promise. He made his way to a warren he knew near the Budby road which he had visited earlier in the day and set a dozen snares in the rabbit runs around it. He was in luck, seven of them had done their job, now he could pay for the arrows and food, and still have food to take with them tomorrow.

It was early evening when Toby returned to the shelter. He carried on his back a roll of hessian sacks, which he dropped on the ground beside Anne. He had three rabbits that just required skinning, which he did in a matter of minutes before handing them to Simon to skewer and put to roast. Anne passed each of them a bowl of the stew they had made earlier and they all sat down to eat.

"Was there any more news?" Simon asked.

"None was offered," Toby answered, "I didn't ask for fear of rousing suspicions, they would have wanted to know why I was so interested. I told the Fletcher's wife that I may be staying in the area for a while, and begged those old corn sacks which can be used as either blankets or bedding. Thinking there may be more rabbits coming her way, she gave them to me. Filled with bracken the ground won't feel as hard. There are six of them, so we could cut three to use as blankets. We can carry them with us when we leave. There is one of her aprons rolled up in them too, she doesn't know I have that, I thought it may be useful to carry cooked food in, to keep it separate from the bread. Could you manage to carry that Anne?"

"Yes of course Toby. There is bread and cheese, and those rabbits you have just caught that we can roast and take with us." replied Anne. "There is some stew left that can be eaten for breakfast. We could eat it cold but, if it is left in the embers overnight, it may still be warm in the morning."

"Spoken like a true country girl," said Toby, "There are cows in the next field, how about fetching us some milk?"

"Fetch it yourself or drink water as I do," she quipped, "because I am not going near any cow."

"Not a country girl yet then Toby." Simon observed.

"No, but she has done well, I shan't complain," said Toby.

"Do you spend a lot of time here?" Anne asked. "You have gathered more pots, bowls and such here than at the last shelter."

"Yes I winter here. I find it safer here when the trees are bare, and there's plenty of game for me to catch." Toby answered. "Though I am hopeful this is the last time I will shelter here. I feel there is change coming, when wrongs will be put right and good prevails over evil. But that is for the future, now is the time to rest, the sun has gone to bed and so must we."

Next morning Toby was up at first light. He rekindled the fire and left. The fire was well lit and the stew hot when Anne and her father came out of the shelter.

"I wonder where Toby is?" said Anne, "He must have left early, I did not hear him leave."

"Toby will be doing what Toby has been doing these past few days, looking to our needs." Simon told her, "He will be back before the sun is fully awake. Let us eat and be ready for when he returns." Anne filled two bowls with stew.

"There is enough left for Toby when he returns, the turnip and beans added to those birds made that stew go a long way, Toby is certainly a good provider, we have never been hungry." Anne commented. "And the sacks made sleeping more comfortable, I slept the whole night. You were right when you said we could not get by without him. He will get us to safety, I know he will, and when he does, I want you to help him with the same resolute enthusiasm that he has helped us with father."

"Yes my daughter, if we get out of this we will owe him our lives. I will never be able to repay him fully, but I will do what I can," he replied.

While they were waiting for Toby's return, Anne put all the food they would take with them into the flour sack, the roast rabbit wrapped in the apron as Toby had suggested. Simon emptied the bedding sacks and rolled them tightly, then tied them as before so that they could be carried as a back pack. When they were ready they sat by the fire and waited. The sun was over the horizon and

Toby had not yet returned. Anne was getting worried for him and was just about to ask her father what they should do when she saw him walking over the clearing toward them. She picked up a bowl and filled it to the brim with the remaining stew, and then took the pot to the stream to wash it.

"Good morning," Toby greeted them as he sat by the fire. "I see you are all ready and eager to leave."

"Oh Toby, you have been away so long I was worried for your safety," she told him. "Eat your food, you must be hungry." Toby picked up the stew,

"You don't have to worry I'm fine. I took more rabbits to the fletcher's wife, and then I've been checking that our way is clear and I'm pleased to say it is. I saw no one, not even a farmer or woodsman all the way over the River Poulter to the Worksop road."

"How far is that?" Anne enquired.

"Not quite as far as we travelled yesterday. But walking will be a little easier as it is mainly oak forest with areas of heath land. How is the leg Simon?"

"It feels better than yesterday; I shall know when I have walked apiece." Simon answered. "If I could walk as you do, we would be safe by now."

"Well you cannot so why rile yourself," Anne argued, "Toby understands, don't you Toby?"

"I do," affirmed Toby. "If we are ready then let's go on. We can rest again when we have crossed the river, and again when we have crossed the road to the east of Worksop. While you rest there I will find somewhere to stay for the night."

They set off once more, making better time today and were soon over the river and heading toward the road.

"How is the leg?" Toby asked.

"It's sore, but I can go on," said Simon, "let us get over the road before we stop. We can eat then if that's alright by you."

"That's fine but don't overdo it, you must say if you need to rest. You too Anne, how are your feet?"

"They are alright, the salt water helped." she answered.

"Good, then if you are both fit we will run the next few miles; No? . . . No I didn't think so . . . Look, you must not overtax yourselves, we may have to run and hide, do you understand? It will be better to be a day late, than get caught now."

"Yes you are right, but honestly we can go on a while longer." said Simon.

"Good." Said Toby, and continued to walk in front. They made good time and reached the road just before midday. Toby went ahead as usual and crouched behind some bushes. They could hear a cart trundling down the road. Toby waited, but this time as the cart passed he ran out and walked behind it, riffling his hands through the sacks in the back of it and putting something in his shirt. Anne and Simon held their breath. What was Toby doing? Surely he would be caught. Then, just as quickly, he jumped into the bushes on the other side of the road. A moment later a smiling Toby, eating an apple, emerged and beckoned them over. When they reached Toby, Anne started to slap his arms and chest,

"Don't you ever do that again, you frightened me to death, he could have caught you!" she said angrily.

"That was an unnecessary risk Toby." Simon agreed.

"No it wasn't," laughed Toby, "I know the man; he is a market trader and is as deaf as a post. He won't miss a couple of apples, here," he threw an apple to each of them. "Come, let's get away from the road and then we can dine."

"Please promise you won't do anything like that again Toby? Please?" Anne pleaded, "It's wrong to steal anyway," Toby didn't answer.

They walked on a while and came to a small stream, crossed over and stopped on the far bank under some beech trees. "We should eat now, and then while you rest, I will go on and find somewhere to stay the night. Perhaps I can steal some more food while you are not watching," he smiled.

"I'm sorry Toby; it's just that you frightened me so. I care what happens to you," Anne pleaded, "I do not want them to whip you or chop off your hand!"

"Alright I'm sorry; I should not have told you those things, although what I told you that is the truth, but I understand what you are saying," said Toby, "now eat your stolen rabbit and we will say no more of it." Anne passed a rabbit to each of the men-folk from the sack, and then started to eat one herself.

"How much further do you think you can walk Simon? I would like to go on a further two or three miles if you can manage it. By the look of the sky the weather could break, I will try to find us some kind of shelter."

"Aye, I'm sure I can manage that at least. The leg has held up well today." Simon replied. They sat and ate the rest of their meal in silence. When he had finished Toby got up.

"You rest yourselves here; I'll take a look around. We are close to the point where Osbert will not follow, but I have learned that desperate men do not always do the expected, so please be vigilant and keep out of sight as much as you can. I should be back in an hour or so."

"We will." said Simon.

"You take care too Toby, please don't take any risks." said Anne.

Toby found the road leading north out of Worksop and followed it a for a mile or so, staying off the road, while skirting the small hamlets he saw on the way, until he came to a small open fronted hay barn nestling in some trees out of sight of the road. On closer inspection he found that it housed a hay cart with a broken axle. There was a little hay in the back of the barn but otherwise it was empty. The walls and roof looked in fair condition. Provided they left early to avoid being seen, this place would give them shelter for the night. Toby decided to go back and bring Simon and Anne here.

He started back following the road south toward Worksop, but again staying inside the edge of the forest, so as not to be seen, as he had done before. When through the trees as he reached the outskirts of Carlton village, he noticed that there were an unusual number of people on the road travelling north. Moving closer he saw they were villagers pushing handcarts, or driving horse drawn carts, filled with their belongings, others were walking alongside carrying small children or bundles. Toby decided to break cover and find out just what was happening. He approached an old man, who was sat on a fallen tree by the side of the road taking a breather, and asked him the meaning of this exodus. What he was told made his heart race. He ran down the road and through the forest, not stopping until he reached Simon and Anne waiting by the beech trees. When they saw Toby running toward them, they immediately thought there was something wrong and jumped to their feet ready to run too. Toby stopped in front of them exhausted, he dropped to his knees gasping for breath.

"What is it Toby, what's wrong?" Anne cried as she sank to her knees in front of him. Simon stood, quarter staff in hand waiting for whoever was chasing him, but no one came. Toby by now had caught his breath.

"Nothing wrong," he gasped. "Good news . . . Osbert has ordered all his men back to their barracks at Ollerton, but most of them have deserted him, they have all left. The Archbishop of York has reached Tickhill in force with other Lords, and will march south in the morning. Fearing the worst, the villagers in their path have packed their belongings and are moving on mass to Tickhill. They think it is the start of a civil war that has been threatening between the Barons and Earls of this land."

"I would draw the line at civil war," said Simon. "But that is certainly good news Toby. It will suffice to drive Osbert from this land."

On hearing this, Toby got to his feet, he was shaking, his face turned white. Simon and Anne saw the joy that was on his face turn to disbelief and anger. He picked up his bow and turned to them. He spoke slowly, deliberately and yet scathingly,

"I will leave you here. Your way is north, you will soon find the road to Tickhill and your friends. No doubt you will then forget Osbert and return to the safety of your home, letting others take the consequences of your actions. Yes, your actions. I cannot let the matter rest, as you are willing to do. There are scores of men, women and children, aye children, who were accused falsely, and died cruelly and needlessly at the hands of Osbert in the name of the King, including your servant Thomas and the priest at Ravenshead.

And will again if he is not brought to justice, do you forget them? They need to be avenged. Osbert needs to be brought to trial and punished for his crimes, not driven out. It seems I must do this alone, or die in the attempt. Granny Smith warned me this would happen, but I didn't listen. She warned that knight would not turn against knight for fear of his own life, now I see the truth in her words. There is no honour or justice left in this country."

"Wait Toby," said Simon, "come with me, talk to the Archbishop."

"To what end? So that you can drive Baron Osbert out, that he can return later even more powerful? And do even more killing in the King's name? I will tell you this, if you do what you have said, when Baron Osbert returns, and mark my words he will, he will come for you. Yours will be the first head to roll. Then there will be civil war, and the good people of England will pay for it, not the Barons and Earls, but the good common people of this land . . . No, I must do the job myself." Toby replied, "Goodbye Anne, remember me."

"Please Toby, listen to my father!" she cried. But Toby had gone into the forest. "Oh father! There is so much hate and anger in him, yet he is such a good young man, what is it that drives him so? You promised to help him; he risked his life for us. We owe him so much I can never forget or abandon him."

"Yes I did, I must show him that there is still some honour left. Come, we cannot help him standing here, we must get to Tickhill, and today, even with this bad leg of mine," Simon replied. "Leave everything, we must hurry."

"Look father, in his haste, Toby has left his rabbit skin coat. I will take it to him the next time I see him."

"Leave it, he has no further use for it." Simon told her as he walked away.

"No I will not," Anne replied. "I will see him again I know it, I will keep it until that day." She picked up the coat and took it with her.

Despite the pain to his leg. Simon and his daughter made good time as they found the road and joined the other travellers heading toward Tickhill and safety.

Toby meanwhile had made better time heading south, he no longer had Simon and Anne to slow him down or use his time tending to their needs. Nor had he need to walk through the forest, he was no longer hiding. He could follow the great road south. Anger and determination spurred him on, he was on a quest, and nothing was going to prevent him achieving his goal.

He reached Ollerton in the late afternoon and walked through the town. There were no traders on the streets and the people were scurrying round. No one on the street stood talking, as normally happens of an afternoon in a busy market town. He continued until he reached the Stag, an ale house which was the local hostelry opposite the old mill. There were soldiers sat outside, all drinking ale, and all slovenly dressed. The miller and his wife were stood in the mill doorway, watching them and shaking their heads, disgusted with what they saw. Toby walked over to them and asked,

"What's happening here, why are the soldiers drinking so heavily, and where are all the townsfolk?"

"Hello Toby, where's your coat? I hardly recognized you without it," said the Miller, "I'm afraid they are not soldiers anymore, if ever they were once; they are deserters waiting to join The Archbishop of York when he gets here. The loyal soldiers have gone to Nottingham with Baron Osbert; they left this morning leaving this rabble behind. Its woe betides any man found on the street when they've had their fill. I am shutting the mill, you should get away too. No good to be done here today."

"I will thank you."

Toby continued on his way, still following the road south and then west toward Glenford. He reached the old shelter very late in the afternoon; he lit a fire and then went off to catch his supper. An hour later three rabbits were roasting on the homemade spits. He ate one and wrapped the others in their skins to take with him. Night was upon him and he was tired. Toby entered the shelter to settle down for the night. As he lay down he felt the sword Simon had left there wrapped in Anne's old dress. He pulled it from beneath the bracken where it had been buried. Feeling the dress material made him once more think of Anne, and the short time they had spent together. He wondered if they had got back safe to Tickhill and the Archbishop of York. Perhaps he had been too hasty and should have seen Simon safely to his friends before leaving. Perhaps he should have spoken to the Archbishop himself. Would he ever see Anne again he wondered. Perhaps . . . All these things were going through his mind as he settled down to sleep. Next morning Toby woke early as usual. He picked up his bow, arrows and the two remaining rabbits and made to leave. Seeing the sword he unearthed the night before, he decided to take it with him; he gathered it up still wrapped in the dress, put it over his shoulder and made his way to Glenford and Granny Smith's house. She was doing her housework and saw Toby come to the doorway.

"Good morning Tobias. What news do you bring? Did you get them both to safety?"

"Yes, I left them north of Worksop yesterday about mid-day," Toby replied. "Osbert's men had all left the area, so it was safe for them to continue on their own. It sounded by the way Sir Simon spoke being safe was the end of it. He just wants Osbert to go some other place. 'It will suffice for him to be driven from this land.' Toby mimicked. He will not help me clear my family name, for all the help I have given him."

"What are you to do now then Tobias?" she asked, "I did try to warn you to let them settle their own scores."

"Yes you did, and now I understand, that knowledge may help me force their hand." Toby answered, "The Noble Lords from the north, along with the Archbishop of York, are marching south from Tickhill Castle as we speak. Osbert will have gone back to Nottingham Castle. The Earl of Gloucester is still there, Osbert will ask for his protection. I hope to be there when the two forces meet. If I may, I will take my father's clothes which carry his crest. They may be a loose fit for me, but I think they will suffice, his belt and dagger too."

"They are yours; you don't have to ask," Granny told him, "they are there in the chest his old servant brought to me." Toby took the clothes from the chest and put them on. "Osbert will think he has seen a ghost when he sees you in those. You are the image of your father, and they fit you better than you thought."

"I have one last favour to ask of you, if you feel you are able." said Toby.

"What is it?" she asked.

"Will you meet Sir Simon de Selis on the Nottingham road and give him this?" Toby held up the sword still wrapped in Rebecca Anne's dress. "It belonged to his father.

It may stir something in him. Enough that he should want to help me when the time comes."

"I will travel with you as far as the Nottingham road; there I will wait for him. But please be careful Tobias; don't show your hand until their Lordships get there." Granny pleaded.

"Let us eat then." said Toby as he produced the two rabbits he had been carrying. "This meal will probably be the last today, as I won't have time to catch more."

"Then take some bread and cheese with you," said Granny. "When we have eaten I will put some in a bag for both of us, I will be coming to Nottingham too."

After they had eaten, she put some things into a large cloth bag and they both set off toward the road leading south toward Nottingham. When they arrived, Granny Smith found an old tree stump where she could sit and wait. Toby put her bag and the sword, still wrapped in Anne's old dress, beside her.

"Take care Tobias," she said, "I hope all will go well for you today." Toby leaned over and kissed her on the cheek.

"I have a feeling it will. I will find you again when all this is finally over." And then as he was walking away, he turned and said with a twinkle in his eye. "Tell Anne I will be waiting for her. I still wear her charm."

CHAPTER FIVE

WHILE TOBY HAD been travelling south to Glenford, Sir Simon and his daughter followed the road north. By mid afternoon Simon was in some considerable pain, still very weak and struggling to continue. Anne was doing her utmost to help him, but was finding the task too much,

"We should rest awhile father," she urged her father. "Just for a short time, until your pain has eased."

"Have you a problem there?" A man's voice called to them. Anne turned to see who it was. A horse and cart pulled up alongside them, the man driving it looked like a trader by the way he was dressed, just like the one whom Toby had stolen the apples from earlier. Alongside him sat a small boy and a woman, Anne took to be his wife and child.

"Yes," replied Anne, "my father has injured his leg and is in considerable pain. We must reach Tickhill today. Will you help us? He cannot walk much further." Anne caught a look of surprise on the women's face. Then saw her put her hand on her husband's arm as if to stop him. He got down from the cart.

"Not a local then? No matter, in these times we must help one another. Come let me help you onto the cart, you can ride with us." The farmer helped them both onto the back of the cart and made Simon comfortable on some old sacks.

"What do you mean, not a local?" Anne asked.

"The way you speak tells me you're not the farm girl you're dressed to be, or else you live on a very fancy farm, not at all like the one I work on. It's alright, we don't want to know who you are, just lay back and enjoy the ride, it's not far to Tickhill."

"Thank you." said Anne as she sat close to her father. Simon being in so much pain closed his eyes, not speaking at all.

It was late afternoon when they trundled into the market square at Tickhill. Simon rested now, looked about him and saw there were soldiers checking and guiding the refugees through the town. The livery they wore was that of Sir Roger his friend. Elated, he sat up and removed his smock. When they reached where the soldiers held up the cart to check it, he called to one of them.

"You there, soldier. Take us to Sir Roger Busli as quick as you can."

"And why should I do that?" asked the soldier.

"He is a friend of mine; I am Sir Simon de Selis. Send someone to tell him I am here, and then take me to him."

"Oh yes, and I'm a court jester! Now get that cart out of here before I put my sword across your back." He replied. Anne jumped down from the cart, and putting her face right up to the soldiers face shouted,

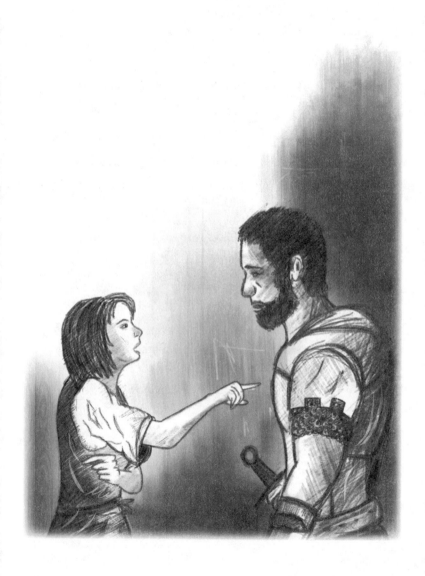

"We have been chased all over the shire by Baron Osbert, lived like animals in hedge bottoms, and had nothing but rabbit to eat for a week. My father is wounded and in considerable pain, and I am tired and dirty and . . . !" She screamed at the soldier. "Now get your captain here at once or I will have you flogged." The soldier froze in astonishment, stunned at the way this farm girl had addressed him. "Now!" she shouted.

The soldier jumped back, turned and went to the front of the cart, returning moments later with his superior.

"This man claims to be Sir Simon de Selis sir," he told the captain.

"I am Sir Simon, or if you prefer Sir Simon de Selis. It is urgent you get me and my daughter to Sir Roger as quickly as possible." Simon told him, then pointing to the farmer on the cart. "And look after my good friend here, he helped me when I could not go on, find him a good place to stay."

"Stay on the cart Sire and follow me. Your friend and his family can stay inside the castle tonight. They can stay in the stables. The Archbishop is already at the castle." Then the Captain turned to the soldier. "You . . . get off to the castle and inform their Lordships, at the double." The soldier left, running as fast as he could to spread the news.

Shortly afterward, the cart was led through the portcullis and into the castle, to be met at the entrance of the great hall by the Archbishop of York and Sir Roger de Busli.

"Good news that God has delivered you alive and safely back to us. How badly are you hurt?" asked the Archbishop. "Come let me help you, and Rebecca what of her, where is she, why is she not here with you?"

"I am here, don't you recognise me?" Rebecca asked as she climbed down from the cart.

"Good gracious what have they done to the pair of you? Are you well Rebecca?" he replied. "They will pay for this outrage." Turning to a servant he said, "Get someone down here to help her, she needs a bath and clean clothes, and some food, and get a healer to tend their wounds." Lady Muriel de Busli stepped forward and took Rebecca's arm.

"My dear girl, look at the state of you!" she exclaimed, "Come with me, we will soon have you clean again. I have clean clothes of my daughters that will fit you I think. Then you must eat, I will get the servants to lay extra places for you."

"I am well thank you. Tend to father, his wound needs to be cleaned and re-dressed, and yes we both need to bathe and put on clean clothes. Thank you My Lady." Rebecca answered, she then turned back to the Archbishop "And afterwards Archbishop, as we eat, we need to talk to you at length about a certain young man who needs our help, and the brutality being heaped on the good people of this shire." Servants came and carried Simon away as they spoke.

"We will. Rooms are being prepared for you, go and bathe then we will talk, where is this young man you speak of?" The Archbishop asked. "I will have him brought here." They walked across the great hall and as Rebecca was led to the doorway she called back.

"We will have to go to him, by now he will be roasting a rabbit for his supper before he goes to sleep in his shelter. Tomorrow he will pursue Baron Osbert alone if we don't get to Nottingham in time to stop him."

"What shelter? What manner of man is this that sleeps in a shelter?" he asked.

"A good one Archbishop, one to whom we owe our lives." Rebecca answered as she disappeared through the doorway.

After they had both bathed and changed their clothes, they met the Archbishop along with three of his senior knights, Sir Roger and his wife, Lady Muriel, for a meal. The Archbishop wanted to know the truth in every detail, of what transpired between Baron Osbert, his brother, and the Earl of Gloucester. And how they escaped and managed to travel the length of Nottinghamshire without being found by Osbert's soldiers. Who helped them, how they obtained food to keep them alive, and where they slept. All at the table sat in stunned silence as Sir Simon told them everything regarding the quarrel he had with the three conspirators, and how he had to fight his way out of the castle when Osbert's brother tried to kill him. How Thomas his servant had taken Rebecca to the stables, found a cart and got them all safely into the forest, before he himself was caught and killed. Rebecca then eagerly took up the story and told them how they met Toby. How he hid them, provided for them, found the clothes to disguise them, found Granny Smith to tend to her father's wounds, laid a false trail to Lord Chester's land, and led them to safety, hiding in hedge bottoms and eating lots of rabbit and sometimes pheasant, which he was very adept at catching, cleaning and roasting. While knowing all the time he was risking his life by helping them. Sir Simon told them of the cruelty and poverty the people of the shire had to endure at the hands of Osbert and his soldiers in the King's name, and how he wished to help them by having Osbert brought to justice for treason.

Astounded by what they had just heard, the silence continued for a moment, the Archbishop then rose to his feet,

"These crimes against the King will not go unpunished; I will have their heads for this outrage!" he then turned to one of his knights, "Sir Guy, the King is staying at Newark, go there and inform him of this, and how they are plotting to take his throne. Tell him that I march to Nottingham at daybreak in his name to clear this nest of rats out once and for all. Then meet me there as soon as you can." Then turning to the other two knights he ordered, "Sir Thomas, take twenty men and go to the Earl of Chester. Inform him of what we are about, and ask him to bring what men he can muster and come in to the west of the castle. I believe his men are already on the border. Ask if he can spare you men to cover the south, and stop their escape. You ride with his Lordship's men to the south and give them what help you can, but be on your guard, I don't trust the noble Lord, he is known to change his allegiances like chaff blowing in the wind. And you Sir Ivan, I would that you do the same with Lord Newark and protect our eastern flank. If either Lord refuses, send me word at once. I will bring the main force in from the north with Sir Roger. Is that all understood, are there any questions?"

"Yes." Sir Simon replied, "Have you forgotten me? Where do I fit in your plans? I shall be riding with you."

"I shall be coming too." Rebecca told him.

"I would have thought you two would need to rest." The Archbishop said, then when he saw the protest in their faces added. "If you can sit a horse, then alright you come too Simon. You Rebecca can travel at the rear with the soldiers' wives, but I would much rather you stay here where it's safe."

"Safe Ugh, after what I have been through? I too can ride a horse and I will ride at the front with my father. I can show you the way if you get lost." she quipped, "Now we should all get some sleep, we leave at first light if that is not too early for you. I cannot wait to get into a nice clean soft bed, goodnight everyone." Rebecca smiled and went to bed leaving the Archbishop speechless. Sir Simon laughed and said,

"You will find your match with that one Archbishop; she has stubbornness about her, and is no longer the girl you knew. I took her to Nottingham as a child; she came back as a woman. I'm afraid the events of this last week have forced her to grow up fast."

"Then I think we should do as she says and all retire to our beds." said the Archbishop. And then turning to Lady Muriel said "Thank you My Lady, for your hospitality."

"It is our pleasure, Sir." she answered. They all left for bed knowing that the events that would unfold tomorrow, will probably change all their lives.

Next morning Rebecca was up before dawn, and dressed in a riding habit that Lady Muriel had found for her. She went down to the great hall where her father and other knights and Lords were waiting,

"Good morning Rebecca, did you sleep well?" Sir Simon asked.

"Good morning father, yes I did, although it felt strange at first. Is the Archbishop not here yet? I thought I would hear him barking out his orders by now. Surely he has not overslept? How is your leg today father?" Rebecca asked.

"My leg is stiff but I can ride, and no, the Archbishop is at his prayers, as he always does before going into battle. Ah, here he is now," Simon answered as the Archbishop appeared.

"Is everything ready?" The Archbishop asked. There were murmurs all around the hall of 'Yes my Lord'. "Then for God and King Stephen let us proceed. I want to reach Nottingham before the sun goes down, so the march will be forced and without rest if we are to achieve our goal. Then we will attack at dawn tomorrow and clear out this nest of ungodly vipers."

Everyone followed him out of the hall and into the courtyard, where they mounted the waiting horses and moved out of the castle, and made their way to the front of the waiting column of soldiers. They moved through the town to the sound of the cheering townsfolk, and down to the road leading south to Nottingham. In awe at the magnitude of the army with which she was travelling, Rebecca rode alongside her father and two of his knights, who had newly joined them from Adwick, just behind the Archbishop and his personal Knights.

"How can anyone resist an army like this?" she asked her father.

"Sir Robert the Earl of Gloucester has an army and Baron Osbert too has men at arms, as you know. A lot of good men will lose their lives this day; this is not an easy task we are about. When the fighting starts you must not argue with me, you will go to the rear of the column and stay there until the day is won, or lost as the case maybe."

"You think we may lose this battle father?" she asked.

"Men always go into battle thinking they will win, we are no different," he answered, "but there is no guarantee, the other side think that they will win also. Don't worry, we have God and right on our side, and the Archbishop is a good commander, I know of none better. We will win the day." Rebecca rode in silence now; her father's words did not fill her with confidence. She looked at the stone faced knights and soldiers around her, no one was smiling, no one speaking, the only thing she could hear was noise of the horses' hooves and the jingle of harness. Just before they entered Ollerton town the column halted, men were sent to check that it was clear of Baron Osbert's men, while the main body of men rested. There was a lot of movement between the Archbishop and the town before the column resumed its journey.

"What's happening father?" Rebecca asked.

"There were deserters from Baron Osbert's force wanting to join us." Sir Simon answered. "You can never trust a deserter. They have been told to prove themselves worthy by travelling in front of the column as an advanced guard, and to open the gates to the city for us to enter. They are in no man's land, in danger of being recognised and killed by Baron Osbert for desertion as they advance, or being killed by our own men if they turn and run. Do not forget, these are the men that have been willing to abuse the good people of Nottingham in the past. They were also the men searching for us these past few days."

Rebecca sat in silence, remembering what Toby had said about power hungry men, and that the fighting and killing would never stop until they were no more, and how he would like to see England change. She was afraid for his life now, being alone in Nottingham. She realized what Toby had meant when he had said he knew what had to be done; but she wished that he had waited and was here with her.

A few miles on from Ollerton, Sir Ivor, a knight who had been scouting ahead came back to the column.

"An old woman up ahead sends a message for Sir Simon de Selis and Lady Rebecca," he announced.

"Then give it to them." answered the Archbishop. Sir Ivor continued,

"She asks that you go to her, as she has something of your fathers to return to you My Lord, and to tell Lady Rebecca it is wrapped in her old dress." Simon and Rebecca looked at one another and said together.

"It's Granny Smith!"

"Who is Granny Smith?" asked the Archbishop.

"She is the healer I told you of, who tended my leg in the forest and provided us with food and clothing." Sir Simon replied, "Take me to her that we may see what she has of mine." Simon and Rebecca broke ranks, brought their horses to a canter and joined the knight in advance of the column. They soon came upon Granny Smith waiting patiently on the stump where Toby had left her.

"Granny Smith," called Rebecca as she jumped down from her horse and went to embrace her. "Are you well, where is Toby? Is he safe?"

"Tobias has gone on to Nottingham. I did try to dissuade him, but after what your father said to him, he thinks he is alone in his quest. He left you this My Lord," Granny said holding up the bundle. "He thought if you were going into battle you would need it to do honour to your family name, as he is trying to do for his." Simon took the bundle from her and proceeded to unwrap it. "He told me to tell you Lady Rebecca, that he still wears the charm you gave him and that he will be waiting for you." Simon un-wrapped the sword, removed the one he was wearing and replaced it with his fathers.

"I will find Toby; I promise you he will not be alone. Rebecca and I owe him as much and more," said Simon. "And you, what will you do now?"

"I will make my way to Nottingham to be with him when he needs me," she answered.

"Then you will travel with us," Rebecca told her. "Father, I will go to the rear and travel on one of the carts carrying the supplies with Granny, can you arrange that please?"

"Yes that can be arranged. We near Nottingham now, and we will camp for the night shortly, then our army will attack the castle at daybreak." Simon told them.

The column had caught up with them; without stopping, Rebecca and Granny were made comfortable on one of the carts, Sir Simon regained his position and they continued their journey.

It was late in the day and the sun was setting as they made camp less than a mile from Nottingham castle. Tents were erected, fires were lit and meals prepared. After the gruelling march the soldiers were very tired. Wives and camp followers tendered to their needs, while servants provided for the Lords and senior knights, a maidservant attended to Rebecca and Granny in a small tent erected beside her fathers. The Archbishop called a meeting of his generals, senior knights and Lords that had joined them, to discuss the plans for battle on the morrow. They let the deserters believe that the advancing army were waiting to be joined by Lord Chester's forces and Lord Peveril's archers, knowing that word would get to the forces in Nottingham castle, who would then be deceived into thinking they would be facing a much bigger army. The forces were camped in an arc around the north of Nottingham. After dark, fires were lit all around at intervals so that the forces inside Nottingham could see the glow of many large camp fires and would think that these other forces were indeed joining them.

The Earl of Gloucester had heard the rumours and at first dismissed them, but as the night wore on, and he could see more campfires to the east and west of him, he began to believe it. When he saw the fires of Sir Thomas being lit to the south, which would cut off any escape route, he decided that the odds were too great. He instructed his senior knights,

"Form my men into groups of no more than ten and slip them quietly out of the south gate at intervals, try to evade the enemy and regroup with me at Kegworth. From there we will head back to Bristol. Do not inform Baron Osbert of our intentions. If questions are asked we are sending out patrols to find the enemy's strength. This battle was of Osbert's making, now most of his own men have deserted him. I will not let my men die in vain to save his hide, let him deal with it."

The Earl of Gloucester and most of his army had escaped before Sir Thomas and his knights to the south had realized what was happening. Only a handful of the Earl's soldiers were caught and killed, but a few of Osbert's men, who tried to follow, were driven back into the castle.

Baron Osbert was furious; his Master at Arms had informed him that the Earl had left only after his own deserters had been forced back into the castle grounds. The deserters were immediately put to death.

Seeing the futility of trying to man the castle walls with so few men, and the castle surrounded, he knew there was no chance to escape. Baron Osbert ordered his loyal guard back into the main building. His plan was to surprise the vanguard of the attacking force by leaving the gates to the courtyard open, luring them in, then he would attack them, while leaving men hidden to close the gates behind them, cutting them off from the main force. This way he hoped to cut the attacking force down considerably before retreating back into the castle where, in the confined spaces of the passageways, his loyal guard could not be overpowered so easily by sheer force of numbers.

CHAPTER SIX

NEXT MORNING AS the sun rose on the camp, Rebecca and Granny Smith were served breakfast, and while they ate they saw men preparing for battle. Wives and children helping their husbands and fathers don their clothes and implements of war. The words of her father came back to her thoughts as she uttered,

"A lot of good men will lose their lives today. How many of these wives will be widowed and how many children orphaned, will the fighting and killing never end?"

"While men lust for power, it never will," said Granny Smith, "avarice, envy and the lust for power is, along with religion, at the root of all wars. Good men die to serve the will of the few who rule us. All that we can do is pray that it will end soon."

Trumpets began to sound, drums rolled, generals barked out their orders, and the advance began with Sir Ivor once more in the vanguard.

The castle was built on a hill. To the north and west there was a high cliff. The main force moved to the east and south of the castle, through the town, and to the main gates. As the force reached the castle walls they expected to find resistance, there was none. The gates were open wide, Osbert's army were nowhere to be seen. The advance party went cautiously into the castle grounds. For a few minutes there was a ghostly silence as everyone held their breath expecting a trap or some other kind of treachery. Then they saw a figure stood at the entrance to the courtyard, all alone waiting for them, his bow on his back and a short sword in his hand,

"Osbert has his elite guard inside the castle, they are waiting for you." He told the advancing knights, "There are a few men hidden here in the grounds. I believe that when you men of the advance party are all through these gates, they mean to close them behind you, trapping you in the courtyard. I have been watching them from the battlements. Those inside number just a hundred and fifty men and are the best he has, in fact they are all he has. Robert of Gloucester left in the night taking his men with him."

"And who are you?" asked Sir Ivor.

"I am a friend of Sir Simon de Selis, a poacher called Toby, who helped him to escape Baron Osbert in the forest a few days ago and as such I would ask a favour."

"I have heard of you, Sir Simon speaks highly of you. Ask away my young friend, and I will do my utmost to oblige," answered Sir Ivor.

"I would have Baron Osbert taken prisoner and brought to justice so that he answers not only to his current crimes but to his past crimes of treachery, treason and injustice against the King and his subjects," pleaded Toby.

"I have heard of your quest. If it is possible I will do as you ask, others here today would want that also, but in the heat of battle it may not be possible. Now stand aside and let us at these elite guards." He turned to a knight beside him, "Take the last ten men, this young man will show you where the treacherous dogs in the grounds are hidden, and make sure to keep the gates open."

Toby moved to one side and let him pass; then with the knight took the ten men back to the castle grounds where, with Toby's help they easily dealt with the ones hidden there. Toby's arrows found their mark, two fell wounded, and two more were dealt with by the soldiers, the others seeing they themselves were trapped between the main force and the advancing soldiers looking for them, fled.

Meanwhile Sir Ivor spurred his advance guard forward. As they made their way through the courtyard itself Baron Osbert's elite guard came out to meet them. The fighting was fierce and bloody. Osbert's guards knew for them it was a fight to the death, there was no escape. They fought bravely, but as more soldiers poured through the open gates to reinforce the advance party and Osbert's hidden men failing to do their job, they were overwhelmed and pushed back into the confines of the castle.

Dead and wounded from both sides lay everywhere. In the narrow passageways the guards held the advancing troops for a time, but by sheer weight of numbers, they were forced back until at last they regrouped in the great hall, in front of a large oak table, behind which sat Baron Osbert on a large ornamentally carved chair. Out of a hundred and fifty elite guards, only twenty were left standing, their blooded swords at the ready, still prepared to fight for their lives.

"Hold!" a command came from the doorway. "Put down your swords, you have fought well, surrender and you will live, not another soldier has to die today."

The Archbishop and his knights strode into the hall. Osbert's guards looked round at him, as though asking for orders. Baron Osbert sat rigid in his chair, not moving, his hands gripping the chair arms so tightly, were white as snow, his eyes were wide open, and he was shaking with fear.

"You will get no help from him. See for yourselves, he has not had the courage to draw his sword," said the Archbishop. "But you have proved your loyalty and fought bravely, for that I salute you, and will spare your lives. For the last time put down your weapons and leave as free men."

The guards looked at one another. Seeing the futility of their situation, one by one they put down their swords. Their captors stood in two lines and simultaneously placed their own swords across their shields in salute to their bravery as they left the building. A cheer went up at the news that the fighting was over and the day was won. Cheers replaced with fear as the womenfolk rushed forward to find their loved ones. That fear turned to wailing and tears by those whose husbands and fathers had given their lives that day. For the first time, Rebecca saw the full horror of war, as she walked between the bodies of dead and wounded soldiers from both sides while looking for her father and Toby.

In the great hall the Archbishop had been joined by all the other Lords and senior knights. For the first time Baron Osbert spoke.

"The King himself will hear of this, and when he does your heads will roll. This is an outrage!" he shrieked.

"We are here in the King's name; to clear out a nest of Vipers who plan to take his crown and give it to Empress Maud. It looks as though some of them have escaped, slithered back under their rocks, but they will be caught and duly punished," the Archbishop bellowed back and thumped his armoured fist on the table in front of him, "How plead you to the charge of treason against the King?"

"It was Sir Simon de Selis who was plotting to take the crown, not I. Where is your proof it was I?" cried Baron Osbert, "It was he, Sir Simon, who murdered my brother, because he overheard Sir Simon speaking of such matters to another."

"You are a liar as well as a murderous, treacherous, treasonous dog," said Sir Simon. "It was I who heard both you and your brother speak of treason in conversation with Robert of Gloucester; you will not shift the blame to me, sir. You had my servant Thomas of Doncaster murdered, so that he could not testify against you."

Gasps and murmurs behind them made them turn. King Stephen had entered the hall,

"I have been listening from the doorway," the King told them, "and it seems to me that proof is lacking on either side, it is one knight's word against another, and I have to decide which of you is telling the truth and which of you is indeed guilty of treason."

He walked to the centre of the hall, but, before anyone could speak. Whoosh . . . thud. An arrow struck the chair above Baron Osbert's head. And a voice rang out.

"I, Tobias le Clerc, son of Sir Roger le Clerc, grandson of Sir Simon le Clerc, accuse you Sir Ralph Osbert, who calls himself Baron, of the false accusation and murder of my grandfather, father, mother and my two siblings, along with ten of our servants, in the name of King Stephen. In that you did unjustly accuse them of treason against the King and, without a trial or evidence of this, you did have your soldiers herd them in to the church at Farnsfield and set fire to it, burning them all to death. After which you did confiscate all their lands and possessions for your own. I am here to see that justice is done and that you answer these charges before the King." Toby stood in the balcony above the doorway, with a second arrow fixed to his bow aimed at Baron Osbert.

"Was that Simon and Roger le Clerc who fought with me in France, and were at my Coronation when I arrived in

England?" the King asked. "I see you wear their crest on your tunic."

"Yes Sire, the very same," Tobias answered.

"And you say they were burnt alive in a house of God?"

"Yes Sire, I do, and in your name," replied Tobias.

"These men were my trusted knights, they would never turn against me, and you say Baron Osbert burnt them alive in a church?" the King asked again angrily, "If you could fire an arrow as well as your father, that shaft would have been through his heart."

A second arrow flew through the air, embedding itself so close to the first, the shafts were touching.

"I can shoot an arrow as good as any man in your kingdom Sire, my father taught me. If I don't get the justice I deserve, the next arrow will be through his heart, but to kill him without trial would make me as evil as he." Toby replied.

"That church burned down three years ago," screamed Baron Osbert. "It was an accident; there was nothing I could have done to help them, I was not there. Once again I am falsely accused; it is a conspiracy against me. Where is the proof?"

"I am the proof!" a woman's voice rang out, "I, Lady Maud, wife of the murdered Simon de Clerc, mother of murdered Roger de Clerk and grandmother of Tobias." Granny Smith stepped forward, "I was there when you lit the first torch and laughed out loud when the church collapsed on my family inside. I lay in the pigsty holding my grandson to prevent him screaming and running helplessly to his family's aid. We both watched as you gave orders for us to be found and killed. The priest there was ordered to Ravenshead church, on pain of death if he told what he had seen. He was murdered when they were hunting Sir Simon de Selis for fear he would help him and bear witness to Baron Osbert's earlier crime. We have lived as fugitives and peasants since that day three years ago. I as healer in a village, and my grandson has lived in hedge bottoms and caught rabbits to make his way, but will do so no longer." Then turning to the King she said, "Sire you know me and my family from our days in France, when both my husband and son fought by your side. We have always been true to you but, if men like Baron Osbert are allowed to make these accusations in your name, not one of your true followers will be safe. Your throne may be in danger my liege, but not from anyone in this hall, apart from Baron Osbert." The King thought for a moment, then turned to Baron Osbert,

"If it was true that these good Lords had wanted my crown for my cousin Maud, what better time than kill me right now? I have no army here but them. I think that Sir Simon de Selis is telling the truth." Then turning to Tobias said, "Come down here Tobias, you will have your justice."

Toby came down from the balcony to be met by Rebecca Anne; she flung her arms round him, gave him a hug and then holding his hand, walked with him to Lady Maud and bowed in front of the King.

"I believe your story Tobias, but I cannot think of a way that justice can fully be done. Nothing I can do can bring back your parents, or your siblings. Come kneel before me." Tobias did as he was bid. The King drew his sword. "I will restore all your titles, along with all the land and property that was taken from you. Your family name will be restored without blemish." The King touched Toby on the shoulder with the sword. "And from this day you are to be known as Sir Tobias de Clerc, Knight of the Realm." The silent gathering cheered, banging their swords on their shields and shouting together, 'Welcome Sir Tobias!'

The King raised his hand. "Take that man out and hang him," he said pointing his sword at Baron Osbert. "Then when everyone has left, burn this castle to the ground with him in it, as testimony to his treason, and may he burn in hell."

Osbert, screaming in terror, was led out to another part of the castle by the Kings own knights, to be hung. The King then turned back to Tobias,

"Who is this young lady by your side, holding you so tightly that she may never let go? Introduce me."

"She is the Lady Rebecca de Selis, daughter of Sir Simon de Selis, whom you know Sire," he replied.

"So Lady Rebecca, why do you hold him so tightly?" the King asked. "And what is that rag you hold on your arm?"

"He left me once before, to come here to this place to clear his name. I hold on to him so that he will not leave me again, Sire," she replied bashfully. "This rag is his rabbit skin coat, his disguise all these years. People of this shire know him by it and think well of him. He left it behind in the forest, it is part of his life, and he should treasure it."

"Well said my Lady. And do you approve of this young Lady hanging onto your grandson, like chain mail hangs on a knight, Lady Maud?" the king asked. Lady Maud smiled and nodded her approval, while putting her arm round Rebecca.

"And you Sir Simon, it looks as though you are soon to have a son in law, do you approve of this also?"

"Yes Sire," he answered, "He risked his life to help me and my daughter when I needed help most, not knowing who we were. I owe him my life. I could not wish a better man for my daughter. I knew nothing about his past until now, yet he has proved to be a brave, honourable and honest man, and has promised to guard my daughter with his life. I know he can keep her well fed with rabbit and clothe her with the skins, build her a shelter in the forest, and is willing to take a switch to her if the need arises. She says she could live like that, if she puts her mind to it, so yes I think he will make a good husband for my daughter."

"Hush father, be quiet!" Rebecca told him, "You embarrass me!" All the Lords laughed.

"But that apart, he is a man of principle and of the people. He knows what it means to live as a commoner, outlaw, fugitive, and peasant, he will give his life to right the injustices done to them by people like Baron Osbert. He longs for the day when England will be at peace, with no more war, a place where ordinary people can live their lives without fear, Sentiments that I agree with."

"Then I know this part of England is in safe hands," said the king, "but first we have to find these people who cause this anarchy and remove them, until then there will be no peace; Sir Ivor will you do something for me?" The king asked.

"What is it Sire?" asked Sir Ivor, "Your word is my command."

"I have made this rabbit catcher a knight, now if he agrees I think he needs to be fully trained in the skills of a knight. What say you Sir Tobias," asked the king.

"I would like that Sire," Toby answered.

"Sir Ivor, you are one of the most skilled knights in my kingdom, therefore

I charge you with this task. Teach him well, I can use a man like him in my service, and I think you are the best man to teach him,"

"You can leave the matter in my hands, Sire." Sir Ivor replied.

"Go and rebuild your family Sir Tobias, and don't forget I want an invitation to your wedding, especially if rabbit is being served for the wedding feast," said the king as he made to leave the hall with his knights. "Sir Ivor, I leave you a boy, nay a young man, bring him to me when you have made him into a knight, the like of his father before him, for I have need of such men." When the king had left, Tobias turned first to his grandmother,

"Now at last we can return to Farnsfield and rebuild our lives. Once more you will command the respect and station in life that you deserve." Then turning to Anne, "Now you understand that things are not always as they seem, I can now show my true feelings toward you." A broad grin came across his face as he continued, "I promise to make you the best shelter in the shire, with lots of bracken for you to sleep on, and you can always use my rabbit skin coat as a pillow. That's if you still feel the same as you did that day in the forest, only with your father's consent of course."

"Yes please," replied Anne.

"Then let's get on. We must get to Farnsfield Manor before nightfall. We don't know what we shall find when we get there after Osbert has done his worst."

"I and my knights will accompany you, to make sure Osbert's men have left before we make our way home," said Sir Simon.

"I too, shall be with you," said Sir Ivor, "after all it will be my home until you are fully trained."

Tobias turned to his Grandmother,

"Come Grandma we have cleared our family name, Osbert is no more, and we are at last among friends, let us go home."

CHAPTER SEVEN

OVER TWO YEARS had passed since that day in Nottingham. The Archbishop had sadly died shortly after returning home from Nottingham. Toby had grown tall and strong in that time, with a mop of brown hair which hung down on to his broad shoulders. Lady Maud had been busy hiring staff and getting Farnsfield Manor back to its former glory, while at the same time helping to plan the wedding for Toby to Rebecca, which would take place three days hence. Rebecca and her father Sir Simon were due to arrive tomorrow, to help put the final touches to the event.

Tobias had been training hard to become skilled as a knight, and Sir Ivor pushed him to his limits and beyond. His young body ached under the stress and pain of the intense training, but he would not ask for quarter. He had the strength of mind to realise that, if he was to be the master of Farnsfield like his father before him, then this is how it had to be. Getting the rundown estate up and running again, in the way his father had in the past was also proving difficult but, it was well underway. The local people saw all this, and warmed to this young man whom they called Young Master, he was proving to be a fair and honest employer.

Sir Ivor saw all this too. As he taught Toby his skills, he had grown close to him. They were now firm friends and, in his mind, even though there was ten years difference in their ages, he felt they were like brothers. They were finishing a practice session with bow and arrow, when Sir Ivor put his arm round Toby's shoulder,

"My work is finished here Toby, I have fulfilled my pledge to King Stephen," said Ivor. "You are as good a knight in every way, as any knight I know. You treat everyman as your equal, no matter their station in life. For this you command a great respect from everyone, Lord and commoner alike. And your skills with weapons are better than most and almost equal now to mine. With the bow you have no equal. I can teach you no more. I will report this to the King. Only practice and experience will teach you more. I must now get back to the King's side, he has laid siege to Lincoln Castle, and has sent word that he needs me. He has sent his apologies for not being able to attend your wedding."

"I understand the King has matters more pressing than my wedding, no apology is needed. As for treating the people as my equal, both I and my grandmother have lived with these people as equals, they are the salt of the earth," replied Tobias. "But they have suffered terrible hardships and cruelty under Osbert. I have seen this with my own eyes, and suffered with them. Now they are being treated both like men and human beings, and deserve to be. They work hard and get a fair return for their labours, as you have seen. I work with them in the fields when it is needed. They fill my barns with corn and put food on my table, when they have problems they come to me. I help them when they need help. Yes, I think of them as my equal, for that they respect me. While I am master of Farnsfield, it will always be this way." He then turned to face Ivor, "Will you delay your journey until after I am wed? You know that it is planned for three days hence. I need you by my side on that day. I have no father to witness my marriage, and we feel . . . that is my grandmother and I, that in these past two years you and I have become close friends, close enough for you to take my father's place by my side. We feel that you are one of the family. I have no one else that I would ask to accompany me on such a solemn a day. The church has been re-built in time for the occasion. We will all be disappointed if you are not there." Sir Ivor thought a moment, then turned to Toby and looked directly into his eyes.

"Sir Tobias." he said formally. "You will never know how much you honour me by asking me to do this. I will proudly stand beside you at your wedding."

"Thank you Sir Ivor," replied Toby. Sir Ivor continued,

"I have spent my adult life in the service of the King, travelling from place to place with him, without roots, no home of my own. Sometimes sleeping in barns and stables and washing in horse troughs, I have no family of my own, they are all dead. No wife, I feel my life is not fitting for a wife and, until now, no close friends. In these troubled times I have trusted no one, and kept my own counsel. I envy you Tobias. Yes I know your life would have been different had your father and siblings not been murdered, but you still have a grandmother, and soon you will have a wife, both of whom love you, and will always be there for you to come home to. You have built a new life here, with servants who love you too. Believe me that is rare in these times. You are the most honest and trustworthy person I know. Now, with God's help, you can rebuild a family. Yes I envy you, and I am honoured, that you wish me to take your father's place at your wedding, but mostly I am honoured that you think of me as family, from now on I shall think of you as my brother. From the bottom of my heart, I thank you. I shall always be there for you, just call and I will come. As for the siege at Lincoln, that will wait, I will leave as soon as you are wed."

While they had been talking, they had been walking back to Farnsfield Hall in time for dinner, as they reached the entrance Toby replied,

"I know that I speak for both my grandmother, and Rebecca my wife to be, when I ask you to please consider Farnsfield as your home, there will always be a place at our table for you." They both went inside to enjoy a meal.

The next two days were hectic, the hall was trimmed, and a feast organized for the big day. Guests were arriving; rooms had to be readied for them and their servants. The great hall was being prepared for the banquet and, not forgetting his people, in the large barn, tables were erected and all the villagers were invited to join in the celebrations. Then at last, all was ready and the big day had arrived. It was a cold February morning, but villagers from miles around arrived at the church, all wishing to see the marriage of their young Lord to his sweetheart Lady Rebecca.

The small Church was filled with Lords, knights and their ladies; the new Priest was waiting to officiate at the wedding, when a loud cheer from outside told everyone the couple had arrived. Toby and Ivor were the first to walk down the aisle to the altar, Toby proudly wearing his family's crest on his tunic, followed shortly after by Lady Rebecca and Sir Simon. Rebecca looked beautiful in the white lace covered gown, much different from the girl in the forest, who wore the clothes of a farm girl and had her hair cut short. Now her hair was long again, her head covered in a bridal veil, as was the custom. But you could still see the sparkle in her eyes and the smile that stole Tobias's heart. The wedding went without a hitch and, as they left the church, the knights in the service of Sir Simon formed a guard of honour, raising their swords to form an archway from the church porch to the lych-gate out of the church yard. As the couple emerged the villagers cheered. Toby, hand in hand with his new bride, decided to walk back to the manor. Children sang and danced in front of them. The lords and knights walked in procession behind them, marvelling that the common people should honour a lord in this way, most common people were in fear of their masters, but here they seem to love him and it was good to see.

When they reached the steps into the manor, the servants were lined up on both sides. Tobias turned and lifting Rebecca in his arms, walked up the steps and through the great oak doors, he said,

"Welcome Lady Rebecca Anne de Clerc to Farnsfield Manor, your new shelter in Sherwood. I hope you will always be happy here." He lowered her back to her feet.

"Oh I will! I will be happy here with you." Rebecca answered. As they embraced, Lady Maud came up behind them,

"You can save that for later Tobias, you have guests to entertain come along." She told them as she led them into the dining hall, where tables were set, and on to the head of the table.

The other guests followed and were seated. Lady Maud and Sir Simon sat on either side of the bride and groom, Sir Ivor sat beside Lady Maud, and the Priest sat alongside Sir Simon. The other guests were escorted to their respective places.

When everyone was seated the Priest said Grace, and asked for God's blessing for everyone present and for King Stephen. Toasts were then given to the Groom and his Bride before then food was served. There was boar, beef, venison, chicken, pheasant, and for the Bride and Groom, Rabbit served on a comfrey platter. When Toby saw it, he nearly choked on his wine with laughter, then saw the humour in it and blamed Sir Ivor for having it served. Sir Ivor denied this saying,

"The King said it should be served, when we were at Nottingham over two years ago, remember? I was only carrying out his wishes."

"I like rabbit," said Lady Rebecca. "They were part of the events which brought us together, without them we would never have met, and this marriage would never have happened."

"Then I will make a toast to rabbits," said Sir Simon. "Without them I would probably have been caught in Sherwood, and both my daughter and I slain. He raised his tankard, "A toast to the Rabbits of Sherwood." The guests all cried together, 'the Rabbits of Sherwood!' The knights banged their fists on the oak tables.

When everyone had eaten their fill, it was late afternoon. The guests were dancing in the main hall, when a servant rushed in and approached Toby,

"Forgive me my Lord. There is a knight outside in the hall. He is wounded, and asks to speak with Sir Roger de Busli regarding the King," everyone stopped what they were doing and looked toward the door.

"Then bring him in, don't leave him in the hallway," ordered Toby.

Sir Roger, hearing the servant, joined Toby as the knight entered the hall, his head swathed in bandages. He looked around, and then made his way to Sir Roger.

"Forgive me my Lord; the King has been taken prisoner by Robert of Gloucester, aided by the Earl of Chester and many Welsh troops." The guests all gasped at this news. "He is being taken to Winchester, where they intend to put Empress Maud on the throne, saying they will go on to take London and crown her there. I heard them say this as they led the King and other Barons away. I am Sir Thomas, knight to Sir William Peveril, who was also taken. They left me for dead." Sir Thomas continued to tell all about the battle and what had happened that day, "All this happened three days ago. I have walked day and night to find you, I could not trust anyone. You don't know who your enemies are anymore."

"You have done well," said Sir Roger. "Go and eat, and then rest, we will talk later." He then turned to the other knights, "We know now who our enemies are. I have never trusted Chester . . . craved too much power and was a law unto himself. Well, the King needs us. I ride for Winchester as soon as I can muster an army, we must free the King. Are you with me?" he asked the lords and knights.

"Yes," they all answered.

"Then I suggest you take your ladies home tomorrow and find as many fighting men as you can, then wait until I call. But first try to enjoy the rest of the evening." he turned to Toby. "Congratulations on your marriage to Lady Rebecca. I think you will make it a good marriage, and thank you for inviting me."

"It was our pleasure," replied Toby. "It is I that should thank you for taking the time to come and be with us on the day of our marriage," replied Toby.

"Yes, I agree," said Rebecca, "but surely you will stay tonight and travel home in the morning."

"Yes, that would be best, I'm not as young as I once was," replied Sir Roger. "Everyone has had a good time here today and it's a pity that it has ended with this bad news. There will be civil war now until King Stephen is released and Empress Maud exiled. What you have done here in these past two years Tobias has given me hope, that the whole of England will be the same in the future."

"Thank you my Lord." said Toby. "Now it is time that we said our good nights and retired to our bedchamber, for we have had a long and tiring day."

"Practice at daybreak?" inquired Ivor.

"Not on your life," answered Toby. Everyone laughed as Toby led his new wife out of the room.

There was an air of both excitement and apprehension as his guests, who were all loyal to King Stephen, stood around and talked, mainly about the news they had received and how it would affect both them and England. But also about Toby and the way he had rebuilt Farnsfield, and how his workers and servants looked to him and loved him. Lady Maud listened and was proud of her grandson, that these powerful lords and knights admired Toby in the same way as they did his father. Now at last she knew that she was home.

Next morning, Tobias and Rebecca were up early, to see all their guests were fed, and safely on their way home, before they themselves, Lady Maud and Sir Ivor, sat down for their breakfast. They spoke at first about the previous day's proceedings, and how they thought it had been a perfect day, spoilt only at the end of the day by the news about the King, on that subject Rebecca asked,

"How long will it take Sir Roger to build his army?" It was Ivor who answered.

"It could take weeks or even months to raise and train enough good fighting men to take on Chester and Gloucester. Together they are a powerful force. I think word would be sent to Queen Matilda, Stephens's wife, to let her know of the Kings predicament. She could muster men to go to his aid. I will wait to see what happens before I make a move. What is your take on this Toby?

"If the King needs me I must go to him," Toby replied. "He is the one who restored my land and titles to me, I am indebted to him. If the King is not reinstated to the throne, then I could lose all this. I don't like the idea of being a poacher again."

"It will not come to that will it Toby?" asked Rebecca. "I would not want you to go to war, but if you believe it to be necessary, then I will stand with you."

"Yes I believe it will," Toby answered, "But thanks to Ivor, I am well prepared, but I don't think it will happen for a time, by then you may be glad to see me go," he added with a grin.

"Toby, how could you say such a thing," Rebecca rebuked him, "I would never be glad to see you go to war. I saw what war did to the men at Nottingham. I would not wish to see you dead. Please do not make a joke about this."

"I would not like to see you or Ivor go to war. We are a family, and have earned the right for a few years of peace and happiness," said Lady Maud, "but if you must go, we both, Rebecca and I, will count the days to your return. This anarchy between the earls and barons, has cost me a husband and a son, I would hate to lose a grandson too."

"Enough talk of war, with its doom and gloom. Come Rebecca let me show you round our estate. This time without having to hide in hedge bottoms," said Toby, as he got up from the breakfast table. "The horses are saddled; we will be riding this time, so your feet won't get blisters." As they left, Lady Maud said to Sir Ivor,

"To think I warned Tobias about getting too close to Rebecca. I was wrong, what a lovely couple they make. They have both worked hard for this marriage; I would hate to see this war break them apart."

"I don't think anything could," said Sir Ivor. "And don't worry, I will look after him if we do go, that I promise."

Toby and Rebecca rode out across his estate, visiting each of the villages that were upon it in turn, and talking to the villagers in them. Rebecca marvelled at the way they were received. There was no one hiding from them, everyone came out to congratulate them on their marriage, wishing them well for the future. One woman even asked Toby when he was going to start catching rabbits again, as she missed her rabbit stew, which brought a round of laughter.

Sometimes Toby would have to act as a Magistrate, or arbitrator in disputes, if the village elders could not deal with it themselves. The greater offenders like thieves, robbers, murderers, were rare on the estate but, when they occurred, Toby dealt with them justly and where needed, harshly. He favoured no man above another, whatever their status in his Manor. For this he was greatly admired. If they had problems, either singly or in groups, they would come to him, he would help to find a solution. With rents and taxes he was fair, and never left them destitute, as their previous master baron Osbert had done. This arrangement suited everyone, and had continued since his titles and land had been reinstated, with the help and guidance in the first year of Sir Simon, and Sir Ivor. Since then, he had taken the responsibilities of office on himself, although still under the watchful eye of Sir Ivor.

———⚫———

It had been almost six months since the day of their marriage, six months of peaceful life deep in the heart of Sherwood Forest. This was the same forest where Toby had once spent almost three years of his young life as a fugitive, in fear for his life, poaching rabbit and pheasant to make a living. Living and hiding in hedge bottoms to escape the clutches of Baron Osbert.

Now with his new wife he was revisiting the places he knew and the people who had befriended him, to thank them. This particular day, he had been visiting the fletcher and his wife at Budby, both to show off his new wife, but mainly to buy arrows for himself and Ivor. On the way home they stopped at the shelter where he first took Rebecca and her father. Looking at the small overgrown entrance Rebecca said,

"How on earth did we get in there, it's so small."

"You were smaller then. Do you want to spend the night here? I'll go and catch supper while you collect wood and light a fire," replied Toby.

"No thank you, I prefer my nice warm bed," she answered. "This place has too many bad memories, although it was the place I first got to know you, and the first place I had feelings for you, so it was not all bad, but no thank you, I would like to keep such things as memories. Now I prefer my own bed in the new shelter you made for me at Farnsfield, which is much more comfortable."

"Come then we have a long ride home." Toby helped Rebecca back on her horse and they both set off for home.

It was early evening when they arrived at Farnsfield Manor. A stable lad came to take their horses.

"Begging your pardon Sir Tobias," he said while taking hold of the horse's reins. "Sir Simon is waiting for you inside, he asked me to tell you to go straight in when you arrived."

"Thank you John," said Toby. "Give them a good rub down and a handful of oats, they deserve it." Then turning to Rebecca he asked, "I wonder why your father wants us so urgently," They walked toward the house and went inside to be met in the hallway with Sir Simon, Sir Ivor and Lady Maud.

"What's wrong? Why do you have such stern looks about you? Has something happened since we have been away?"

"I'm afraid so." Sir Simon was first to speak, "Sir Roger has sent word that Queen Matilda, King Stephen's wife, has formed an army made up of mercenaries from Flanders, and the loyal people of Kent. The people of London have also formed a militia, and together, they have driven the Empress out of London. The Queen is planning to pursue her until her husband is released and is now set to march on Winchester castle with a thousand men. She will need all the help she can get; Sir Roger will be leaving at once with thirty cavalry to support her. He has asked if you would accompany Ivor, find the Queen and tell her what Sir Roger is planning to do." He then added, "He wishes you to leave at daybreak tomorrow, which does not give you much time to plan your journey."

"Ivor and I have readied ourselves for this day since the King was captured, we will leave at first light," replied Toby. "But I would ask you a favour. I know Rebecca and my grandmother are capable of running my estate, but I would ask you to keep an eye on them in my absence, some would take advantage of a woman?"

"You don't have to ask, she is my daughter, I will make sure they don't come to any harm. But come, you need to eat." They walked to the dining room, where Toby and Rebecca sat down to a meal.

"I will tend the horses, and collect what we need for the journey," said Ivor. "Perhaps you will find the route the Sir Roger is taking, if we run into Chester's men, we can ride back to warn him. I will see you at daybreak Toby. To the rest of you I will say my good bye, I will return here when the job is done if I may?"

"You had better or I will be vexed. You are now regarded as one of the family, this is your home." Lady Maud scolded. "We will all be there to see you off in the morning. You can say farewell then, never goodbye. And that will be after breakfast, you must eat before you leave on such a journey."

"That is right," agreed Rebecca. "We could not let you go without seeing you off."

Ivor left, everyone else sat quietly until the meal was finished, Toby pushed his platter away.

"Now Simon, tell me the route we are taking,"

"I have it on a parchment in the form of a map, which you can take with you. It is the most direct route, taken from the records we have in the Minster at York. How accurate it is I am not sure, but you will be travelling the same way as Sir Roger he has the same map. Sir Roger has travelled that way in the past." Simon told him, "Ivor has had four horses shod, and checked the harness, you will need two horses to carry your armour, food and so forth. Everything is ready I think, what you both need now is a good night's sleep."

"I have instructed the servants to pack food, enough to last you both a week if you are frugal with it," said Lady Maud.

"It seems that everyone has been busy except me, thank you," said Toby, "I hope I can make you all proud of me." He took his grandmother in his arms and gave her a hug.

"You just come back to us, that is all we ask," she told him.

"We are proud of you now," said Rebecca. "You look after yourself and don't worry over us, we will be fine, just do what you have to do, then come home as fast as you can."

"Then it's time for bed, goodnight, we will see you all in the morning." Toby and Rebecca retired for the night.

CHAPTER EIGHT

Toby and Ivor were in the stables long before dawn, harnessing and loading their horses ready for the journey. The rest of the household were also up and about getting the meal ready for the pair to have before they left,

"We are ready," said Ivor, "all we want now is breakfast, a change of clothes, say our farewells and then we will be on our way."

"I am not looking forward to the farewells," replied Toby, "I expect there will be tears aplenty, but I have worked up an appetite so we had best go in to breakfast."

"It will be a first for me," answered Ivor. "No one has ever waved me away to war, or anywhere else for that matter, but I will feel it inside of me today. This is a good place, and a good family that we are leaving, and so I too will not be looking forward to leaving. I have been happy and content here." No more was said as they went in for breakfast.

Lady Rebecca and Lady Maud joined them for breakfast. It was quiet; an uneasy silence hung around the table, no one spoke until the meal was finished. Toby was first then to speak,

"Thank you, that was a good meal, but I am afraid it is time we changed to leave, we have far to go this day." He rose from his seat.

"I will help you," offered Rebecca. "I have laid your clothes out on the bed ready for you." When Toby left to change, Lady Maud turned to Ivor.

"I had your clothes laid out too. Please look after yourself and return with Tobias. Perhaps after this the fighting will stop, and then we can have peace."

"I hope so Lady Maud, I will return when the King is free, and has no further need of me," replied Ivor. "Thank you for your hospitality these past years. I too, like Toby, feel as though I am leaving my family behind, thank you for making me welcome."

"You are leaving your family behind; it is a family which you can return to at anytime." She put her arms around Ivor and with tears in her eyes gave him a hug. He then left to change his clothes.

Toby had changed and was now wearing the tunic he wore to his wedding over his chainmail, with his coat of arms, a great oak, across his chest; his father's sword was by his side, and a dagger in his belt.

"You look so handsome!" exclaimed Rebecca, as she put her arms around him. They held on to one another a few moments, before Toby said,

"I must go now, I can't put it off any longer, you know that my darling."

"Yes I know, but in my heart I wish you to stay. Please be careful and come home as soon as you can."

They walked together, to where the horses were waiting. All his servants had come to wish the pair good fortune. Ivor was already mounted. Toby turned, hugged and kissed his grandmother then Rebecca in turn. Rebecca, with tears rolling down her cheeks, tried to cling on to him, her father and Lady Maud gently pulled her away. Toby mounted his horse, then turned saying,

"Farewell my love, I will be back before you know it," and then to his friends and family, "Farewell everyone." This was echoed by Ivor as they both spurred their mounts and rode away.

The gathering stood and watched until the pair rode out of sight, with tears running down the cheeks of the ladies, and jaws clenched tight by the men folk lest they should shed tears themselves.

It was now noon, the sun was overhead, and neither knight had spoken since leaving Farnsfield.

"We have travelled a good way," said Ivor, "let us find a place to sit and have a bite to eat. Yonder haystack looks promising, the horses can have a bite too, I'm sure the farmer won't mind." They steered the horses toward the stack and dismounted.

Tobias looked into the food bag and found a parcel of meat. Wrapped around it was the necklace which Rebecca had made from her hair, complete with the rabbits foot.

"What have you there," asked Ivor.

"A necklace made from Rebecca's hair," answered Toby. "She fashioned it from the hair I cut from her head while I was leading them to safety through Sherwood, I had forgotten it. She gave it to me to wear as a good luck charm."

"Then you should wear it, we may need its good luck before we are through." Tobias put it around his neck.

"Sorry I have been quiet Ivor," said Toby. "My mind has been on what we are about. I hope I don't let you down when we are in the thick of it."

"You will not let me down Toby. I saw how you stood up to Osbert and the King in Nottingham, since then you have been trained by the best, me. You are twice the man you think you are, no, you will not let anyone down, believe me. Your woodsman skills will also be valuable; when we get hungry you can catch me a rabbit," he laughed.

"Don't laugh too much, it may come to that one day, I just hope I haven't forgotten how."

"I have been quiet also; I have had a heavy heart. No, not thinking of what we are about, my mind has been thinking of what we have left behind. Now for the first time, I know why I have been fighting all these years. It is so that everyone, from the King to the lowly commoner, can live their lives without fear, in peace and happiness, as we have done these past two years or more. You, Tobias, have given me the answer I have been searching for. Now when I fight I have a reason other than to please my King. Farnsfield and all it stands for."

They sat awhile at the bottom of the hay stack enjoying their food. When they had finished they climbed back onto their horses and proceeded with their journey, stopping occasionally to water their mounts and stretch their own legs. At night they sought the help of local farmers, slept in hay barns and such, and paid for oats to feed their horses. Some farmers were pleased to share their meals with them, seeking no payment. At other times, especially when they were getting close to Winchester, they just slept out in the open, making a fire to keep them warm, and taking turns to sleep, so as not to be caught by any of the Empress Maud's men who may have been in the area.

At last they came to the outskirts of Winchester. It was mid afternoon when they met a knight of Gilbert de Clare, named Sir Charles. He was with men guarding the rear of the Queen's forces, and was known to Sir Ivor from previous battles. He introduced Sir Tobias to Sir Charles and told him why they were there. He in turn informed them that Bishop Henry, King Stephen's brother, who supported Empress Maud against his brother at first, had changed sides and persuaded those still loyal to King Stephen to join him in his residence at Wolvesey Castle, which had a newly built keep, at the south eastern end of the town. Empress Maud occupied Winchester Castle to the south west. She was angry that the Bishop had changed sides and laid siege to Wolvesey Castle.

Bishop Henry escaped and went to London to persuade the Queen to free his men. Queen Matilda had followed the Empress from London with a large force, surrounded the whole town, laid siege to it trapping Empress Maud between the two forces. This meant there was now a siege within a siege.

Sir Charles also told them that the London Militia part of the Queen's army, who were following from London, were running wild, ransacking all the villages for miles around, burning them down and taking everything of value.

"Where is the Queen camped?" asked Ivor. "I must speak with her."

"Follow the road and shortly you will see the Queen's Standard, you will find her there," replied Sir Charles, "Good to see you again Sir Ivor. Pleased to meet you too Sir Tobias, I'm sure we will meet again soon."

With that the pair rode on toward the Queen's camp. Toby had never seen a town besieged before; he looked around as he rode through the numerous camp fires, each with men that were either eating, just lying around talking, or training. He was surprised that no one had challenged them as they rode right up to the Queen's tent. Only then did a knight come forward to ask,

"State who you are and what business you have here."

Sir Ivor answered.

"I am Sir Ivor of Boulogne, knight to King Stephen and my fellow knight is Sir Tobias de Clerc, newly knighted by King Stephen at Nottingham. We have word of help coming from the north for The Queen."

"Dismount and wait here," the knight ordered. He then turned and went into the tent, coming back out shortly saying, "The Queen will see you. I will have someone tend your horses, follow me."

They both followed the Queens knight into the outer tent. There were two more knights inside standing each side of an opening into the rear of the inner tent. Moments later the Queen appeared through the opening, both Sir Ivor and

Sir Tobias immediately went down on one knee, bowing their heads and saying simultaneously. "My Queen."

"Get up, get up," said the Queen. "What news have you?" The pair got to their feet.

"Sir Roger de Busli is marching south as we speak with thirty mounted men and thirty or more foot soldiers. They should arrive tomorrow and will be at your service my Queen," answered Sir Ivor.

"How far have you travelled to get here?" the Queen asked.

"We have travelled form Nottingham Your Majesty, Sir Roger comes from York," he replied.

"Then why were you not with your King at Lincoln when he was taken? I am sure he could have used those thirty cavalry and thirty foot soldiers then, or were you hiding like cowards after fleeing the field to save your own skins?"

"No your Majesty, I was near Nottingham when we heard that the King had been taken, fulfilling a task he asked me to do for him."

"And what was this task you were asked to do that was more important than protecting the King."

"That is unjust!" Tobias could no longer hold his tongue. "Sir Ivor is no coward! He has served King Stephen well over a number of years. He was training me in the art of war and the skills of a knight at the King's command! There are none better or more loyal in this land than he." The queen was taken aback by this outburst.

"He did not teach you manners whilst training you. In the presence of your Queen you will speak only when you are asked. How do you know there is none better than he, have you seen him in battle?"

"I beg your pardon for my outburst Your Majesty, and no I have not seen him in battle. I was told this by your husband the King, when he asked Sir Ivor to train me. It was the King who also told me that Sir Ivor was always in the vanguard of his army. He would not be trusted to be there if he was a coward." he answered.

"Please forgive him, he is young, but he learns quickly and will prove himself in the service of the King," interrupted Sir Ivor.

"How good is this young knight? In the heat of battle, will he stand or run? Would you trust him with your life? Because that is what you may have to do."

"Yes I would trust him with my life; I believe he is close to my equal with most weapons, and even better with a long bow. He is usually controlled in his actions and is not normally quick tempered. He has seen men accused wrongly before however, and has suffered the consequences. He was just trying to protect my honour, as I would his." answered Sir Ivor.

"Then we can use you both. When Sir Roger arrives I want you to camp on the road to the west. As soon as my army have rested, and the rest have caught up to us, we will storm the town," said Queen Matilda. "If this treasonous Empress Maud and her followers manage to escape, they will try to get to Gloucester and then on to Bristol. I want you to hold them as long as you can, trap them between our two forces. I expect Robert of Gloucester to try to get Matilda away, he is a formidable foe. I will chase him all the way to Bristol if I must, but if we beat him here then his army will turn and run."

"We will do what we can my Queen. We will be spread thinly to guard all the roads out of town but, if they do escape, we will try to hold them," answered Sir Ivor.

"Good, that is all I ask," said the Queen. Then hearing raised voices outside she asked, "What is all the commotion out there?"

"Someone has set fire to some of the houses in town," replied one of the Queens guards. "Fire arrows have been seen coming from Wolvesey castle. It appears that the Bishop's men are purposely setting fire to the town."

"The fools, in this hot weather it could spread throughout the town. What do they hope to gain from this?" asked the Queen. "It may force Gloucester's hand before we are ready. Send word around that we must be in a state of readiness to attack. If Henry's men mean to use these fires for cover while they try to escape from Wolvesey we must be ready." The Queen turned to Sir Ivor. "Go to meet Sir Roger, tell him what I have told you, and hasten him to cover the West road. I hope he is not too late."

Ivor and Toby left the Queen and made their way to the North road, where they once again met Sir Charles. The light was fading as they rode toward him,

"Sir Charles," Sir Ivor called to him. "The night is drawing in and we have ridden far, we need to rest. May we sleep by your campfire tonight?"

"You are both welcome to share our fire; I will find you something to eat whilst you tend your mounts, then you can tell me of your visit to the Queen."

They dismounted, unsaddled, watered and fed their horses before returning to the campfire. Charles had found them supper and ale to 'wash it down with,' he said. They talked of the Queen and of her plans, and of their allies the London militia who were robbing and plundering the countryside, before laying their blankets on the ground and retiring for the night.

Next morning, just before dawn, Toby and Ivor were saddling their horses in readiness to find Sir Roger, when Sir Charles approached them.

"We have hot stew in the pot if you wish to join us; it will warm you before your journey."

"Thank you we will," said Ivor. "It may be the last today if Gloucester decides to break out. I wish that Sir Roger were here now, I would like to be on the West road early, I have a feeling that he will break today. I do not want to miss it riding the countryside looking for Sir Roger."

They sat round the campfire, eating their food, when Charles spoke.

"If Gloucester does try to make a break to the west, he has to fight his way through the Queens army. If he does make it, by that time he will only have a token force with him. If it will help, I can send a man to find Sir Roger. I will leave five men here. The rest, including myself, can accompany you to the West road. Which would be a force of seven mounted men to hold him until your Sir Roger gets here, what do you think?" Ivor thought for a while,

"There are a lot of ifs, and I will give you another. What if he does break through and has twenty or more men with him? We would be greatly outnumbered. Don't forget he will be guarding Empress Maud, her personal guard will be with her too."

"We could at least slow them down, either until Sir Roger gets there or the chasing soldiers catch up to them," Toby interrupted. "I think it is worth a try. In order to free the King we must take the chance."

"Very well, it seems I am outnumbered. Send your man to find Sir Roger, then we must ride," Ivor conceded.

Charles went to talk to his knights, they all wanted to go with him and so they drew lots to see who would be left behind. The ones who had been chosen quickly saddled their horses, the rest grudgingly settled back to what they were doing. First to leave was a young knight on his way to find

Sir Roger, then Ivor and Toby, followed by Sir Charles and his knights. As they rode toward the West road, skirting the many camp fires as they went, they began to see flaming arrows crossing over the town, then a glow as the thatched roofs of the houses caught fire. The cry went up of 'Be on your guard', to all the forces that were besieging the town.

"We must hurry, things are beginning to happen, we must get to the road," called Ivor.

He spurred his mount on, the others followed. The sun was well over the horizon by the time they came to the road leading to Bath. They turned in a line to face toward Winchester, about one mile distant. From there they could clearly see the main gates to the town. It looked as though the whole town was burning. Suddenly men poured through the gates led by Reginald of Cornwall and the fight had begun.

At first they moved forward out of town, then they split, some going left and others turning right, initially taking the Queens army by surprise, but as they pushed forward they soon found that they were outnumbered, but they fought fiercely, leaving a path between the two advancing arms of Cornwall's men. This was Gloucester's chance; he came out of the town at the front of his men, breaking his way through the soldiers who were closing in behind Cornwall's men. Gloucester had managed to almost get clear when William of Ypres and his mercenaries charged into them, smashing his rearguard and chased the rest of his force to the west. Unseen by William of Ypres, Gloucester and around twenty men escaped but, unknowingly, they were riding straight toward Ivor, Toby, Charles and his knights.

"Come we must hold them here," ordered Sir Ivor drawing his sword, and leading the way. "Stay close to me Toby and remember all I taught you."

The small force charged toward the advancing Knights. The first clash was frightening for Toby. Until now he had been following in Sir Ivor's footsteps, now he was on his own in the heat of battle. They took down three of Gloucester's men by sheer force, now it was hand to hand combat. Gloucester shouted to one of his men,

"Get Matilda out of here, we can deal with these." His force split, and ten men rode away, leaving eight men for Toby and his friends to face. Ivor was fighting with Sir Robert of Gloucester when his horse fell; Sir Robert took advantage and trampled him with his own horse then turned toward Toby, who had just slain one of his knights. Toby, now full of controlled anger after seeing Ivor trampled, met him head on, the force of his sword across his head knocked Sir Robert out of his saddle, and he crashed heavily on the ground and lay still. Toby turned again to see two knights attacking Sir Charles. Without thought for himself he rode alongside Charles and with one blow to the neck dispatched one of the knights, he then turned toward the other, who checked, then wheeled around and rode away. Two others still mounted followed. Toby looked around, only Charles, who was slightly wounded, and two of his knights were still able to fight.

"I am going to find Ivor," said Toby, "I suggest you find your comrades, they may need your help." Toby rode back to where Sir Ivor fell. He found him sat propped up against his dead horse. He had managed to remove his helmet and some of his armour. Toby gave a big sigh of relief to see him alive.

"Thank God!" he cried as he jumped from his horse and knelt beside him,

"I thought you were dead. How are you, any broken bones?"

"No, I don't think so. Bruised chest and legs where I was trampled. I must have passed out for a while, when I came too you had gone, but I could still hear the fighting. Did they get away?"

"Not all of them, we accounted for at least eight including Gloucester," replied Toby, "He fell close to you. I gave him a blow to his head, he fell motionless, he must be dead."

"Look for him, we must take his body to the Queen." said Ivor.

Toby looked around; he saw three bodies laying a short distance from Sir Ivor. One of them had highly polished armour which glinted in the bright sunlight. He was laid face down. Toby moved closer, he remembered that Sir Robert of Gloucester wore such armour. He bent over to turn the fallen knight on to his back so as to identify him. When he touched the knight, he suddenly turned over, rose on one knee, sword in hand and slashed at Toby. Toby too quick to be caught that easily drew his own sword and, in one movement struck Sir Robert on his helmet with the flat of his blade. As he fell back to the ground Toby put his foot on Sir Robert's sword and put his own sword to Sir Robert's throat shouting,

"Yield or die?"

"I yield, I yield!" screamed Sir Robert.

"Then get to your feet and remove your helmet, and if you make one wrong move I will kill you," Toby told him. "And don't think I won't. I saw you trample my friend when his horse fell. You gave him no quarter. You also hid like a coward among your own dead pretending that you were dead also, so you could make your escape later, so don't expect to get quarter from me."

"Who are you?" asked Sir Robert, "I have not met you before."

"I am Sir Tobias le Clerc," he replied, and no we have not met." They walked back to where Ivor was waiting, "Now sit there and do not move," he ordered.

Sir Charles, who had been looking for his fallen knights, rode up to where Toby was tending to Ivor.

"My fallen men are dead; my knights are bringing them to the church in Winchester. I caught a loose horse for you to take Ivor there, but I see he can take himself. And who is this? Does he need a horse too?"

"This is Sir Robert of Gloucester, and no he can walk." declared Sir Toby, "He stays in full armour, that way he will not run. Keep your eye on him, he is treacherous and without honour."

"Sir Robert himself! You have captured a powerful man, the Queen will be pleased," quipped Sir Charles.

"Look who comes," said Toby. "A little late, but Sir Roger has arrived," they turned to see Sir Roger and his knights riding toward them.

When they cantered up to Toby and his friends Sir Roger asked,

"Well Sir Tobias, where is this battle we have ridden so far to join, don't tell me it has already ended?"

"No it is not ended and will not end until the King is free," replied Toby. "There will be plenty more battles to win before then. Meanwhile we have to take our prisoner, Sir Robert of Gloucester, to the Queen."

"Then we will set up camp here and wait until my foot soldier's catch up to us. I will accompany you when you go to see the Queen to find how she will use me," said Sir Roger. "I have no doubt she will be continuing to follow the Empress until the King is free and will have need of me. I will provide a horse for Sir Robert if you wish."

"I would have him walk in full armour so that he cannot run, but if you wish he can remove his armour, and be tied to his saddle," replied Toby. "I will lead him and if he tries to make a break I have my bow, he would not go far with an arrow in his back."

"Well said Toby," said Ivor. "Although he is not chivalrous, we are, and if you can take a pheasant in flight at fifty paces with your bow as I have seen, I am sure you could easily take a man out at that distance. Help me mount my steed and then we will find the Queen."

Toby helped Sir Ivor into his saddle, while Sir Charles and Sir Roger tied Gloucester to a horse with his hands behind him and his legs to the stirrups. As they travelled toward Winchester Sir Roger spoke,

"How was your first taste of battle Sir Tobias was it how you imagined?"

"I had no idea what it would be like, but I think it was a skirmish rather than a full battle. I think it went well. If you had arrived a little earlier, I'm sure we would have taken Empress Maud too." replied Toby, "I am pleased that I did not go to look for you myself or I would have missed it."

"Had he not been there we would all have lost our lives," interrupted Sir Charles, "He proved himself on the field; without doubt I owe him my life,"

"That is true," said Sir Robert, "I have seen none better this day."

"Praise indeed when it comes from your ally and enemy alike," said Ivor, "and this is the knight who said he was afraid he would let me down. From what I hear you have earned your spurs today, I am proud of you."

"Thank you Ivor, all the pain of my training has been worth it," replied Toby. "But I was not alone, Sir Charles and his knights were there too, two of them lost their lives. If we had been here on our own against twenty or so knights, we too would be dead. We fought together one for another as comrades should, I am also proud to know such men. I salute them."

By this time they had passed through the battle field outside the town gates where the dead were being collected and the wounded being treated. When they passed through the gates they saw even more devastation. They came up to the castle which now had the Queens guards at the entrance. As they approached they were challenged by a knight,

"What is your business here," he asked.

"Sir Roger de Busli, Sir Ivor, Sir Charles, and Sir Tobias, we are here to see the Queen with a prisoner," said Sir Tobias.

"Who is this prisoner, and why does it take four knights to bring him?"

"The prisoner is Sir Robert of Gloucester," he replied, "and we have other business with the Queen, she asked to see us after the battle. If you would inform her majesty that we are here," the sentry turned saying,

"Follow me." They followed through the courtyard where they dismounted and, after untying the prisoner, were led into a room and asked to wait. The Queen promptly appeared; every knight simultaneously fell to one knee and bowed their heads except Sir Robert. Seeing this, Tobias rose and putting one hand on his shoulder, stamped his boot into the back of his knees shouting,

"Pay homage to your Queen, you treasonous dog," Sir Roger sank to his knees.

"Thank you Sir Tobias," said the Queen, "The rest of you get up, get up. No not you Gloucester, you can stay on your knees like the dog you are. William of Ypres told me that Gloucester's forces surrendered at the bridge over the River Test at Stockbridge, where did you find him?"

"We saw William of Ypres attack the rearguard of Sir Robert's forces and chase them toward Stockbridge. We met Sir Robert about a mile outside the city walls; he and about twenty men were fleeing the city and split from the main group. We were only seven in number," said Sir Ivor. "When we attacked they split up. We then faced Gloucester and eight of his men, we were still outnumbered. My horse fell and I was trampled by Gloucester's horse and lost consciousness. Sir Charles can tell you the rest of what happened."

"Yes my Queen. Sir Tobias fought with Sir Robert while my knights and myself attacked the rest, I found myself fighting two of them when Tobias came to my aid. Due to a blow onto my arm, I was unable to lift my sword and felt that I was sure to die but, as I said, Tobias came to my aid, he killed one knight then turned to face the other, who was by then filled with fear, turned and ran. All of our knights fought well and accounted for six of the nine who faced us, two ran in fear and one, Sir Robert, was captured. Sir Ivor was injured and sadly two of our brave knights lost their lives. That is our report to you my Queen." Sir Charles stepped back.

"I am sorry for our loss. Good and true knights have lost their lives all because of this man," she said pointing to Sir Robert. "So Sir Tobias, you have proved to me that you do stand and fight. Sir Robert keeps only his best knights around him, so to best him and his personal guard speaks highly of you. You have made him prisoner, so what pray shall we do with him?" Sir Roger spoke first,

"Put his head on a lance and parade it in front of our army as a warning to others who stand in our way."

"No," said Sir Toby, "that would give Empress Maud reason to do the same to King Stephen. He is Maud's half brother is he not? How much does she care for him, enough to exchange him for the King?"

"You not only fight well, but you have a wise head on those young shoulders too. If you were Maud, which way would you choose the crown or your brother?" asked the Queen, "Maud may think we would keep him imprisoned and then free him by force when she rebuilds her army."

"I would choose my brother before the crown," said Tobias. "But I am not Maud. Without Sir Robert, she has no army, and what few men she has will not withstand your forces now. Sir Robert's and Sir Reginald of Cornwall's armies were soundly beaten this day, the rest scattered. She needs him to command what she has left."

"Well spoken my young knight," said the Queen, "Sir Roger, you and your knights will wait at your camp until I send word to you." Sir Roger left.

The Queen then turned to Sir Tobias, Sir Charles, and Sir Ivor. "You three will take word to Maud; I will have my scribe write the terms for you to take with you. That is if you are fit to ride Sir Ivor?" She asked.

"Yes my Queen," he answered.

"Then go to the kitchens and tell the staff to prepare you a meal, I will send for you shortly. You can leave at first light tomorrow, find Maud wherever she is hiding and give her my message. When you have an answer, you report to me personally with all haste. Try to find out where they are keeping the King.

If she answers 'no' to the exchange, then we will attack that place and level it to the ground. Until then we will bury our dead and, in three weeks when we are again organised, I will move toward Gloucester and await your return. Meanwhile this treasonous excuse for a knight, who should be put to the sword for his crimes against the King, will be chained and put in the dungeon to await his demise. Guards take him down." The Queen's guard took Sir Robert away. Sir Ivor turned to the Queen,

"My Queen, your word is our command," answered Sir Ivor.

The trio left the Queen and made their way toward the kitchens.

"Look what you have landed us in," laughed Ivor, "The three of us to face the Empress and her army. I think we should surround them, what do you say Charles?"

"No, a frontal attack is in order, with Sir Tobias in the vanguard, after all it was he who got us into this and we are both wounded so we cannot lead."

"Well said Sir Charles, I agree, that is settled then," said Ivor.

"I'll wager you two cripples will be in front at the dinner table, no holding you for that battle," answered Toby.

They reached the kitchens and asked the cook to make them a meal at the Queen's command. With a lot of grumbling, 'I don't know where the Queen thinks I can get the food from she knows we have been under siege,' etc, etc. Eventually the cook did provide them with a meal which, because they had not eaten since daybreak, did ravenously devour,

"We had best find our horses and bed them down for the night," declared Ivor. "They too require feeding; we must tend them and then seek a bed for the night ourselves." Rising from the table they made their way through the castle to the stables where they found a stable boy had already unsaddled their horses, rubbed them down and fed them. Hay had been stacked at the far end of the stalls.

"I think we can sleep well tonight," said Toby, "the stable is warm and we should not be disturbed by our enemies. Your bruises will feel better after a good night's sleep too."

"That's true," replied Ivor, "If you will help us both to get out of our chainmail, we can get an early night. You on the other hand will have to wait for the Queens summons. Did you forget the Queen said she would send for us when her scribe had put her terms onto parchment? As you have just said we need the rest more than you."

"Thanks for that, and who is going to help me with my chainmail when I return and you two are snoring?" asked Toby as he helped first Charles and then Ivor with their garb. Just at that moment a messenger came from the Queen asking them to meet her in her state room. Toby left with the messenger and was led to the room. He was announced and entered into the Queens presence where he knelt on one knee and bowed his head. Before he could say anything the Queen spoke,

"Get up. Where are your comrades I expected the three of you?"

"Apologies my Queen, my friends are both bruised from the battle and need to rest before the journey we are about to take." he answered.

"Very well, but are you sure they will be able to complete the task?" she asked. "Your King, my husband's life could be in your hands."

"Yes my Queen, they will be better for a good night's sleep, by morning they will be as good as new."

"Then take this scroll to Maud, it describes my terms for the exchange of my husband for her half brother. It must be put in her hand alone you understand? Her answer must be brought back to me with all haste."

"I can speak for the three of us my Queen, we will do as you command," promised Toby. He took the scroll, bowed his head and made to leave, when the Queen called,

"Wait one more thing which concerns you alone. One of my commanders, William of Ypres, believes that as he was the one to whom Gloucester's army surrendered, he should be the one to take credit for capturing Sir Robert. What say you to that Sir Tobias?" Toby thought for a moment then replied,

"Others on both sides saw me capture Sir Robert. I cannot see what purpose it would serve, other than to keep him and his forces on your side. But if he needs to take the credit for someone else's deeds to boost his ego, then let him. It will not change the fact that it was I, but it means nothing to me. I just want to see my King released from his imprisonment and back on the throne with you. Word is that Sir William fled at Lincoln to save his own neck, please be wary my Queen, he may run again if the going gets tough."

"Thank you Sir Tobias, I will take heed of your words. I need to keep my commanders happy, but there are few men I trust completely, that is why you three have been chosen for this task. This will not pass unnoticed I assure you."

With that Tobias left the room and made his way back to the stables, where he told his two companions what had occurred.

"I understood that William of Ypres was a great knight, this makes me wonder what other deeds he has to his credit that have been accomplished by others, it is not honourable, the man is without honour," said Charles.

"There is not a lot of honour left in this kingdom," retorted Ivor, "Toby has learned that the hard way in his short life, I know he must have a good reason to allow this, for he fights against this kind of injustice." Toby removed his chainmail and lay down on the hay.

"Let him take all the credit, men on both sides know the truth, and the truth always comes to the surface. The Queen wants to keep him happy; he is a powerful man and is better kept close. I want just to see the King free, and then go home to my family." His two friends nodded their agreement, and settled down to sleep.

CHAPTER NINE

AFTER A GOOD night's sleep the intrepid three saddled their horses, donned their chainmail, put their heavy armour onto the packhorses, and rode out of Winchester shortly before dawn, hoping to reach the camp of Sir Roger just as they were taking their morning meal. It was a cold morning with a cloudless sky. As dawn was breaking the night's frost glistened in the early morning sunshine. The camp fires had been stoked and looked inviting as they rode toward them. Men were rousing themselves to face the new day when they came to Sir Roger.

"Good morning Sir Roger," said Sir Ivor. "We are on an errand for the Queen and thought perhaps you may spare a little of your food to help us on our way."

"Gladly." he answered. "Climb down and join us then while you are eating, you can tell us what is happening."

The three knights dismounted and were each given food, when they were settled Sir Roger asked,

"Now tell me how long we are to wait here, we cannot stay too long or we shall have no food for ourselves."

"The Queen will send you word shortly," answered Ivor. "We three are to find Empress Maud and deliver a message. You and the rest of her army will be following us toward Gloucester. The Queen intends to exchange Sir Robert for the King or, if she refuses, take the fight to her, even to Bristol if need be. She will not stop until the King is free."

"I do not envy you your task," he replied, "Empress Maud may not like the idea and take you three prisoner, or worse. Have you food for your journey, we can spare a little?"

"Thank you, we would appreciate all you can spare," said Ivor. "We don't know how far or how long we have to travel," They finished their meal, accepted a parcel of food each, mounted their horses and bade Sir Roger farewell as they set off on their quest.

Riding hard with only one stop for food and to water and feed the horses, asking directions from farm workers and villagers on the way, they made good time and reached Oxford before nightfall on the second day, where they took shelter in a farmer's barn for the night. The next morning before dawn, the farmer's wife saw them saddling their horses and invited them to share a bowl of mutton broth, which they eagerly accepted. When they had eaten their fill, Sir Ivor thanked her for the meal and offered her payment, she refused by saying,

"No thank you sir. I can see you are not knights of Empress Maud, they would not have asked for shelter; they would have come into our home and slept in our beds leaving us to sleep in the barn. At least you have manners; we can spare a little broth for honest travellers."

"That is good of you," answered Ivor. "No we are not Maud's men. We are knights in the service of Queen Matilda, although we are looking to meet the Empress today at the castle here in Oxford."

"Then you will be disappointed," she told them. "My husband was ordered to take a pig to the castle yesterday just before you arrived. He came home late and told me he did not receive any payment for it. He was told that he should be pleased that he was feeding the Empress and her entourage which should be payment enough. He overheard them say the Empress felt she did not feel safe in Oxford and that they would travel through the night to Gloucester. They left last night, and good riddance to them. Had I known you had dealings with her, I would have told you last night."

"Then we must be on our way. Thank you for your hospitality. We may require the use of your barn again when we return this way. Be assured, we will make payment for your hospitality." Sir Ivor replied.

The three knights left the farm and following directions given to them by the farmer's wife, they were soon on their way toward Gloucester.

"Tell me Ivor, the past few nights have been extremely cold, do you think the Empress would have travelled on without a break for food and warmth?" Tobias asked, "And if not, where would she find shelter?"

"I don't know Toby," he answered. "We have found shelter in farm buildings, so can she. Like you I am a stranger in these parts and don't know of more comfortable places to stay. Even if they did stop, I am sure they would be moving again by now. I don't think we will catch up to them on the road; we cannot travel any faster than we are, we have to think of our horses. They have carried us a long way and although they don't complain they must be tired. No, I think that they will reach Gloucester long before we do. But it will do us no harm to be on our guard."

While they were riding on toward their goal, passing through hamlets and small homesteads, Tobias could not help but notice the fear and despair etched onto the faces of the people they met on the way. The sun was high overhead when they stopped by a stream to water and rest the horses, and to take a bite of food themselves. Dressed as they were in doublet and hose, topped off with chainmail, they were feeling the heat.

"How can it be so hot in the day yet so cold at night?" asked Charles. "I do not like this heat,"

"It is better like this than it be raining and cold," answered Toby. "Empress Maud will be feeling the heat too. We may catch up to them before they reach Gloucester if she needs to stop for refreshment more often."

"Then we must be wary, for they will have left men to guard their rear," said Ivor. "We don't know how many men she has with her. If she did not feel safe at Oxford, then she could be travelling with just a few men. We do know that ten knights were with her when she escaped from Winchester, but we can't be sure."

They decided to stop to feed and water their horses for they were feeling the heat too, and to have a meal themselves, after which they rested in silence for an hour or so before resuming their journey.

Shortly afterwards as they were coming over the brow of a hill, Toby, who was in the lead, stopped and turning to the others said,

"Down there by the stream, there are two men at arms watering their horses, do you see them?"

"Yes, I don't see more than the two. They must be Maud's men. I can't think of a reason for men at arms to be here otherwise," answered Ivor. "You two come in on their flanks. I will be the bait and ride down the hill, getting their attention. If they see only one of us they may not run when I come up to them. Then you come in from each side but slightly behind them." Toby and Charles nodded their agreement and rode off to each side. Ivor gave them time to get down the hill and round behind them, before riding down to meet the two men. As he approached, the two men saw him and mounted their horses, while looking about them to make sure he was alone.

"Good day to you," the first man greeted him. "Are you lost? Where are you bound? Perhaps we can guide you on your way?"

"What makes you think I am lost?" asked Sir Ivor.

"It is unusual to see a knight travelling alone in these troubled times. There is always danger even for a knight that someone would want to relieve you of your purse." The second man answered.

"Are you that someone?" asked Sir Ivor.

"That depends on who you are and what you are doing here," he replied.

"I am Sir Ivor of Boulogne and I am here on the King's business. I am not lost. I intend to catch up with Empress Maud who is running to Gloucester after her army was defeated at Winchester. Now perhaps you will tell me who you are and what you are doing here."

"We are part of Empress Maud's personal guard," answered the second man, drawing his sword as he spoke. "You must get past us if you intend to pursue my Lady any further."

"Would you lay down your life for her?" Ivor asked.

"It is your life that will be forfeit today I think, you are one against two."

"Against two," called Charles.

"Make that three," said Toby as they rode up behind them. The two men looked startled as they turned to face the new threat, "Throw down your weapons or lay down your lives, which is it to be." The two men at arms threw down their swords. "Now dismount and stand very still." As they dismounted so did Charles, who picked up the discarded swords and then took the reins of the two men's horses, led them a short distance away and tied them to the bough of a nearby tree along with his own, Ivor and Toby then dismounted and confronted the two men.

"We intend to pursue Maud wherever she goes, but you can make our journey that much shorter by telling us where Maud is," said Ivor.

"We will never tell you we would rather die first," said one of the men.

"That is foolish," replied Ivor, "To take your lives will serve no purpose. We carry a message from our Queen Matilda for Empress Maud, concerning her half brother Sir Robert of Gloucester, who is imprisoned in Winchester awaiting his demise. Now do you think Maud will be pleased if we told her that you prevented us from delivering this message and because of that, Sir Robert had been executed because we did not get back with her answer on time? Tell me your names so that I can report this correctly."

"My name is Ernst; my colleague is John, what do you want us to do?"

"You, Ernst, will ride to Empress Maud and tell her to wait for us so that we can deliver our message to her in person. We will not deliver it to a third person, impress on her that time is running out for her brother." He then turned to John, "You, John, will lead us to her, and you will take us through the sentries without blood being spilled on either side. Do you have any questions; are you clear in what you are to do?" Both men nodded 'Yes'. "Then we go on." Ernst picked up his sword mounted his horse and rode away at a gallop. John was allowed to pick up his sword too, mounted his horse and led the three knight's on toward their goal.

The rolling hills had become steeper, with cliffs rearing up out of long wooded valleys. John led them on in silence for the next half hour before stopping to inform them.

"The building you see yonder is the farm house in which the Empress is resting; there are guards around the farm who will challenge us as we arrive."

"Lead us on, we will deal with the guards when we get there," answered Ivor, "If Ernst has done as we asked, I don't think that they will bother us."

They rode up to the farm house and were met by one of Maud's knights. Toby looked about him, apart from Ernst who was standing outside the farmhouse door, the knight and John; he could see no other guards,

"Who carries this message for my Lady?" The knight asked.

"I do," answered Toby.

"Then give it to me and I will take it to my Lady when she is rested."

"No Sir Knight, we have been charged with bringing the message to Empress Maud and to put it in her hand only, which is what we intend to do."

"Then my Lady will see you alone," he turned to Ivor and Charles, "you two will wait here."

"No Sir Knight," answered Toby. "We have each been charged with handing the message to your Lady in person. You go to your Lady and tell her we wait here for her."

"My Lady is not at the beck and call of any knight of Stephen or his wife. Why should she come out to see you?"

"If she wishes to save the life of her half brother she will come. If not we tell Queen Matilda that she refused to see us, then what do you think the Queen will do? Go now and bring her to us, or we ride away and the devil take Sir Robert." Toby said angrily. "And there had better not be treachery here, we three must take the answer back to our Queen together." The knight looked shaken by Toby's outburst; he turned and went back into the building. Toby turned to Ivor,

"I see no guards; I presume they are in the building. By going in alone they hope to split us up making it more difficult to defend ourselves."

"You may well be right," replied Ivor. "I would think she has more than the one knight and just two men at arms to protect her. We two will dismount to meet her, while Charles will stay mounted just in case there is treachery here." Having passed the message on, the knight returned.

"My Lady will come to see you at her pleasure," he advised, "but she is not pleased."

"It matters not that she is displeased, it only matters that she receives the message from us and then gives her answer," Ivor answered. "We will wait only a short time. If she delays us, then it may be too late to save her brother, please point this out to your Lady Maud. Queen Matilda will strike for Gloucester on the morrow, and then on to Bristol. Your lady has no army to stop her, both Sir Robert of Gloucester along with Lord Reginald of Cornwall were soundly beaten, their armies mostly killed. The few that survived scattered. Lady Maud would prevent more bloodshed if she were to act swiftly so that we are able to return in time with her answer."

"I hear you," Lady Maud appeared from the house, with three more of her knights in attendance. "Where is this message you have for me?" Toby stepped forward, bowed his head and produced the parchment from his doublet and handed it to Lady Maud. As she began to read it her face glowed red with anger at first and then, as she continued, the colour drained from her, she became white as snow.

"The woman leaves me with little choice." She turned to the knight nearest to her, have the men ready to leave this place within the hour,"

The knight turned and walked toward a large barn standing about sixty paces to the right of the farmhouse, where he called to his men who were hiding there, and told them to get ready to move. Lady Maud was reading the parchment over again and again, until finally she turned to Toby. "Tell that usurper from Boulogne that I will speak to her on my terms at Oxford, I expect all hostilities to cease until after our meeting, is that understood?"

"You have lost your armies, and all your generals, how can you dictate the terms of the meeting?" asked Toby. "My Queen wants your answer in writing, so that no part of it can be lost in translation. We will wait until it is ready, and then if you wish, your knight can accompany us to make sure My Queen receives it with your seal intact. We three give you our word that he will be safely returned to you."

"Mmm, I should have your heads cut off and sent back to her, for speaking to me thus. Wait here," The Empress turned and beckoning her knights to follow, went back into the farmhouse.

Only John the man at arms guarding the farmhouse door, the same man who guided them to the farmhouse was left within sight.

"I'm getting hungry," said Charles, "Do you think if we ask nicely they may give us a meal?"

"You are always hungry," replied Ivor. "Ask John if he can rustle something up for us, and ask also if there is hay and water for the horses."

"I will ask, you should stay mounted, I don't trust this Empress," said Toby as he walked up to the door and asked John. "Would you ask if there is any food we could have, or at least hay and water for the horses? You have no need for a guard we will wait patiently for Empress Maud's answer."

John turned and called though the open door, Ernst came to see what he wanted. The message was passed on and Ernst went back inside. A short time after two men came from the barn, each with a bundle of hay enough to feed all their horses. Soon after, a woman came from the house with three bowls of stew.

"Are you the farmer's wife?" asked Toby.

"Yes sir I am," she answered.

"Do not collect the bowls until both we and the Empress have left, there will be payment in one of the bowls for your generosity."

"Oh thank you Sir," she answered, and then returned to the house.

They had finished their meal, the horses were fed and watered. Charles had dismounted to eat his meal and they all sat under a chestnut tree relaxing in the afternoon sun, when movement just inside the house compelled them to get to their feet. First a knight came out, followed by Empress Maud and two more of her knights, they walked up to the waiting trio, the Empress spoke,

"Here is my answer for her you call Queen. Take it." she said thrusting a parchment into Toby's hand. "My seal is on it. Matilda should be the one to break it. Before Toby could speak she had wheeled round and with her knights gone back into the house.

"We have a few hours of daylight left, I am sure we can make it to the farm where we stayed last night, and then with an early start tomorrow we can reach Winchester before nightfall," declared Ivor. They mounted their horses and set off on their return journey.

"It seems Maud must trust us," Toby remarked, "She has not sent her knight to escort the message."

"That's an escort we can well do without," replied Ivor, "We can rest easy at night." They travelled at a good pace until they reached the same farm at which they had spent the previous night. The farmer's wife met them at the front of his house.

"Good day to you, your business with Empress Maud has been completed I take it?"

"Yes it has, we return to Winchester but, for tonight if we may we would rest in your barn again," answered Ivor.

"You may and welcome. I will see if I can find you a bite to eat while you unsaddle your mounts."

"You are very kind," answered Toby, "but this time we will make payment for your generosity."

They dismounted and first led the horses to a trough for them to drink, and then to the barn where they were unsaddled and given hay. They had just finished tending to their horses when the farmer's wife returned with three large bowls of stew and a loaf of bread.

"I hope you like it; I'm afraid I have nothing more to give you," she said as she handed them to the three men.

"This is fine and very welcome, thank you," answered Toby, "without this we would go hungry until we reach Winchester."

The farmer's wife left and the three men sat in the hay and ate their fill; they then removed their chain mail and lay down to rest. Toby sat up.

"I am going to have a look around, won't be long," he said. He took his spare bow strings and his bow and then disappeared into the twilight. It was dark when he returned, without a word he settled down with his friends and went to sleep. Just before the sun came up, he rose and woke Ivor.

"There are three rabbits on my saddle; they are ready to roast, if you will make a fire. I will be back before long." He went out of the barn and then disappeared behind it. He returned just as the food was ready to eat.

"You haven't lost your touch then Toby," said Ivor. "I'm going to enjoy this."

"Where have you been this morning?" Charles enquired.

"I intend to enjoy one also. No, I haven't forgotten how to catch them. It brought back some good memories and reminded me why I am here. This morning, I thought the farmer and his wife would like a couple, so I have been out to catch more. I have hung four of them on their door and I have three for our journey." While they were eating the farmer's wife came into the barn,

"Thank you for the rabbits, we haven't tasted roast rabbit for a long time, we will have a feast today," she told them. "I suppose you will be off now, so thank you and goodbye have a safe journey." She started to go out of the barn but Ivor called her back.

"Wait good lady, take this," he gave her two coins. "This will pay for your hospitality and enough to buy a pig to replace the one stolen from you."

"You have no need to do that, you did not steal the pig," she told him.

"Then let us call it payment for the use of your barn, the food you gave us and the hay for our horses. No argument, let that be an end to it," he told her forcefully.

"Thank you sir," she answered. Then clutching the money tightly she left the barn and returned to the house.

The three men finished eating, saddled their horses and continued on toward Winchester. They had been riding about an hour when Tobias stopped, turned his horse and listened.

"What is it Toby," asked Ivor.

"Someone is following us," Toby answered, "I noticed earlier the sound of horses' harness, I thought I must be hearing things but I have just heard it again, it seems when we stop, they stop, they must be following us or they would keep moving."

"You say they, how many do you think there are?" asked Charles, "I haven't heard a thing."

"I would say two, perhaps three. You don't hear them because your mind is on the kitchen maid at Winchester."

"I have not heard them either, my mind has been far away too," said Ivor.

"How did you know I was thinking about the maid," asked Charles. Toby and Ivor looked at one another and laughed.

"Because you never think of anything else unless it's another maid," Ivor answered, "They can't be that far behind us. When we get over the next rise Toby and I will hide, you go down the other side, rattle your harness as though the three of us are still riding. Try to keep out of sight, we will wait until they pass us, then come up behind them."

They rode over the hill and halfway down the other side stopping by some overgrown gorse bushes that were dense enough and high enough to hide men on horseback. There was a stream at the bottom of the hill and a stand of trees, which the track they were following ran in to.

"You go on Charles, cross the stream and go into the trees. We will wait here out of sight," Ivor told him. "And don't forget to rattle your harness." Charles rode down the hill rattling his harness all the way, crossed over the stream and went into the wood.

Toby and Ivor did not have to wait long before two horses passed by, the men riding them were talking and laughing with one another. To make sure there were only two men; they circled the gorse bushes and came round behind them. Then riding up behind them as though they were part of a patrol, so close the noses of their horses were nearly touching the tails of the horses in front without being noticed. When they reached the stream the soldiers stopped to water their mounts, Toby pulled up alongside the on the left, and Ivor did the same on the right.

"Good day to you John, and to you Ernst, what is your business here are you lost?" asked Ivor.

"What! Where did you come from? No we are not lost," replied a startled Ernst. "We are ordered to follow you, find where Sir Robert is being held and report back to Empress Maud."

"What will Maud do with this information?" asked Ivor.

"She would send men to free him before she released the King," offered Toby. "Is that not so Ernst?"

"I don't know, we were told to follow and report back if he had been treated properly, if he could ride and where he is being held. We don't know what the Empress intends to do, she would not tell us would she. We are less than dirt to her."

"Then why do you stay with her?" asked Toby, "you can run away, she does not own you."

"Yes she does," John told them. "We have to serve her or our families would be put out of their homes, or even put to the sword, we would like to leave but dare not."

"Would you leave if I told you I know how you could keep them safe?"

"Of course we would, but where in England is safe in these troubled times? Ernst asked.

"Then here is what you must do," Toby told them. "Camp here tonight, in the morning you go back to Maud and tell her that Gloucester is imprisoned at Winchester Castle, heavily guarded by William of Ypres and his mercenaries. Then leave her as soon as you can, get your families and make your way North. You should be far away before Maud misses you. When you have travelled just beyond Nottingham Town, you will look for a place called Farnsfield Manor; ask there for my wife Lady Rebecca. Tell her that I Sir Tobias has sent you and that I am well and will be coming home soon. She will find you work and shelter until I return. But know that it is a long and arduous journey. Will you both do this for your families' sake? I assure you they will all be safe there." Ernst and John looked at one another for a few seconds, John spoke to Ernst.

"If we take our horses I could go back to being a ploughman, and you may find work as a blacksmith again, what say you, I am willing are you?"

"Yes," replied Ernst eagerly. "It will be a new life for us all, but we must guard our tongues when we return, if we are found with even a smile they will suspect something. We must return late and look tired and miserable when we give Maud our message." He turned to Toby. "Thank you for giving us this chance, we will not let you down and we are hard workers."

"Then we will leave you here, take care and I will see you in Sherwood," said Toby.

"Where is Sherwood?" Ernst asked.

"Where my heart is, north of Nottingham, you will know it when you arrive there." Toby told them. Ivor and Toby rode away, leaving them in high spirits for the first time in years.

"That was a goodly thing to do Toby," Ivor commented. "I just hope that they can keep their feelings under control and their mouths shut when they go back to Maud, otherwise they could be dead men."

"They know what they must do. With their family's lives at stake I am sure they will do what is necessary. They are ordinary men forced into Maud's service, and without pay I'll wager, they deserve better."

"That maybe true, but there are many like them, you cannot send them all to Nottingham."

"I know . . . But those two did help us, without their help we could have had a fight on our hands that we may not have walked away from," replied Toby. "They will not find it easy to travel all the way north and with their women and possibly children, food will be scarce and shelter will be hard to find. No I believe if they do get to Farnsfield, they will have shown that they are dependable men and be an asset to the manor."

They rode on and soon came upon Charles who had made a fire and was roasting the rabbits that Toby had caught.

"Making lunch so soon Charles, we have not long since had breakfast?" Ivor asked. "But then I suppose you are hungry again. If it's not women then its food, how do you find time for anything else?"

"They are the two main things in life; anything else is a pastime which I tolerate," Charles answered. "Do you want this roast or not?"

"Yes I want it. If I said no then you would only eat it yourself," replied Ivor.

"Come Toby, get your roast before he makes a pig of himself and scoffs the lot." The two friends dismounted and sat round the fire. Charles passed them their food then asked,

"Who was following us; did they give you any trouble?"

"No," replied Toby. "It was John and Ernst on a mission for Empress Maud; they left on a mission for us. If there had been twenty armed men you would have wanted to eat your fill before you came to our aid."

"It shows how much faith I have in your ability to look after yourself," Charles replied. "If you had been defeated I would not have wasted a morsel of this tasty meal, I would have ate it all, yours too. Then I would have taken you back to Winchester hung over your saddles. Don't you know that in every battle there is always one person that escapes?"

"It's nice to know we can rely on you." Ivor told him. "You can put out the fire and then we ride for Winchester before I roast you on it."

The three then mounted and again started out for Winchester. They rode hard without stopping, except to water the horses and reached Stockbridge late in the afternoon. As they crossed the bridge, Sir Roger's men were still camped there. They rode through the camp toward Winchester, looking for Sir Roger, but could not see his standard. Ivor asked a knight where he was, the knight answered that he was scouring the countryside looking for food, as they were running very low. Ivor thanked him and then carried on to the Castle. As they rode through the castle gates they were met by William of Ypres,

"Hold there," he called. What business do you have here?"

"We are on the Queen's business," said Toby.

"And what business is that, no one passes here without my permission."

"I have my Queen's permission to bring her a message from Empress Maud. I was told to put it in her hand alone, and that is what I intend to do."

"Why you young upstart, you are nothing but a messenger," he said drawing his sword. "Give it to me, I am Sir William of Ypres the Queens right hand, I will take the message to her."

"No you will not! You took the glory for capturing Gloucester from me; you will not take this message from me." Toby leapt from his horse and drawing his sword confronted Sir William.

"A young whippet like you capturing Gloucester, don't make me laugh," said Sir William.

"I did not run from him as you did at Lincoln, and I will not run from you. Stand aside!"

"You had better heed him Sir William, for he did defeat Gloucester in single combat and more of Gloucester's elite guard too. I was there," said Ivor. "The Queen picked him to be the messenger for that reason, so if I were you I would stand aside and let us pass or you may die this day, it is your choice." Sir William thought for a moment.

"Well what is it to be," Toby thundered at him, "I am not in the habit of keeping my Queen waiting."

"Very well you may come alone; I will take you to the Queen." uttered sir William.

"We three were sent on the errand, and we three will take Maud's answer to the Queen," Toby told him. "Now for the last time stand aside, or use the sword you are holding for we are coming through." Toby moved toward Sir William, who put up his sword and stepped aside, allowing Tobias and his friends through.

Leaving their horses with a guard, and giving instructions to have them fed and watered, they moved on into the castle. Sir William watched as they left, shaking with rage after being made to stand aside in front of his men by this young upstart. Toby led them down a corridor to the room where he had met the Queen before; the door was guarded by two of the Queen's knights.

"Inform the Queen that I, Sir Tobias, Sir Ivor and Sir Charles are back with a message from Empress Maud, and are awaiting her pleasure." One knight turned and went into the room, the other barred the doorway.

"Be wary Toby, you have not made a friend of Sir William, he could make trouble for you with the Queen," Sir Ivor warned. "He has her ear."

"I know, but I also know that the Queen does not altogether trust him, she has told me as much." Toby replied.

The door opened, the knight beckoned them inside and told them to wait, and that the Queen would attend them shortly. They went inside. The room was quite large with two doors, the one they had just come through and the other rather larger on the opposite side. The windows on one side were stained glass as you would expect in a church, depicting both knights and bishops, the other walls were covered by drapes, except for two paintings, but Toby could not make out who they were. Chairs were lined around the room, placed against the walls for those waiting for an audience with Her Majesty. After a short time the large doors opened and the Queen appeared with two of her most loyal guard. The three friends got up from their seats and on bended knee bowed to the Queen.

"Get up; let us have none of that nonsense. You have a message for me?"

"Yes my Queen," Toby rose and handed the parchment to her.

"Did she give you any trouble?" the Queen asked.

"None that we could not handle," said Toby. "I had no knowledge of the contents of your message to her, but as she read it she went into a rage. I thought her head would burst as at first she went the colour of blood newly spilled from a mortal wound, and then as the blood drained from her face she turned as white as snow. Let me say she was not pleased, my Queen. She did start to make conditions for the exchange. I told her that she was in no position to make conditions as her armies had dispersed and that you and your army were heading toward Bristol, where your husband was being held."

While Tobias was talking the Queen was reading the message,

"Thank you Tobias. Maud has agreed to the exchange. I have one more task for you," said the Queen while beckoning her knights to leave. "This is to be kept between us only and not to be spoken of outside this room, the walls in this place have ears, I can trust no one. Gloucester is being held at Rochester. With him are ten of my most trusted men, I want you three to leave at first light and bring him to me here. He is to be exchanged for Stephen in two weeks time so ride hard, but be careful; there are those who would kill him to give Maud an excuse to murder Stephen, which would leave the way clear for her son Henry to claim the throne. Take this," she gave Toby a ring. "This is my seal, show it to my men, they have been told not to let Gloucester out of their sight until they see this ring, and that the man carrying it has my trust. My first knight is Sir Geoffrey of Boulogne, he is in charge seek him out."

"I know him," declared Sir Ivor. "He trained me when I was a young man before I came to this country. You will find none better, or more honest and faithful your Majesty; it was he who brought me into the King's service."

"Good, you know who you must deal with. Go now get some food into you; I swear you have all lost weight since I last saw you. Take one of the guards from the door to show you the way, and to get you food for your journey. Don't forget you have less than two weeks."

"Ample time my Queen, we are honoured to serve you," said Toby. As the Queen turned to leave, Tobias stepped in front and opened the large door for her. They bowed their heads and left by the door which they entered, and made their way to the dining room, where they ate their fill before making their way back to the stables. Their horses had been tended, so all that was left was to remove their chain mail and boots, and then settle down to a well earned sleep.

CHAPTER TEN

MORNING CAME TOO soon for the intrepid three. Wearily rising, they saddled their horses and made their way out of the castle grounds. As they passed the gate sentry they were asked,

"Where are you three going at this hour, the sun has not shown his face yet. What is your hurry?"

"We are going home, our work here is finished," replied Toby.

"But the king is not yet free. I would have thought you would stay until the exchange is complete."

"Sir William is here to see that all goes well with the exchange, he does not need us. He will want the credit for this as he does for everything else. Empress Maud is finished, so he should not have any problem. Good day to you."

"Good day to you Sir, have a good journey home," replied the sentry.

The three knights rode on away from the castle, heading north at first before turning east toward Rochester. After they had travelled a fair distance, Toby stopped and turned to Ivor,

"You two ride on, I will go back a little way to see that we are not followed, that sentry was much too interested in what we were doing, I may be wrong but I would rather make sure, I will catch you up."

"I saw nothing wrong," said Charles, as they rode on.

"Toby has had years of being hunted and has developed a mistrust in soldiers. If his senses tell him to check, then I for one will trust him. Let us ride on a while then wait for him to catch up." They rode on not speaking, but with more vigilance than before.

Toby rode back a short distance, seeing no one he moved into some trees and hid there, looking and listening for any sign that they were being followed. After a short time he decided there was no one after all and rode on to catch up with his friends. The rest of the journey went without incident; they slept at night under what cover they could find, not wanting to ask anyone for shelter. They were regarded with suspicion by the villagers they passed on the way. Many running in terror when they rode by for fear, thought Tobias that the army which had marched from London, looting as they marched, had returned. The oppressed people they saw, reminded Toby of the villagers who he had lived with as a child and wondered if their lives would change after the King was freed, as he had changed the lives of the people living and working on his manor, but sadly he did not hold much hope for them.

They reached Rochester late in the afternoon without incident and made their way to the castle where Lord Gloucester was being held. Sentries stopped them at the gate, one of them asking what business they had there. To which Ivor replied,

"Tell that scoundrel Sir Geoffrey that Sir Ivor is here on the Queen's business, and is not to be kept waiting if he is not to be chastised as I would a child. And be quick about it."

"I'm sorry Sir Ivor," answered the sentry. "But Sir Geoffrey is ill and cannot leave his bed, but I will tell one of his knights that you are here and wish to see him."

"Better still take us to him," said Sir Ivor, "we have travelled a long way to see him, and get someone to tend our horses if you would, we will be staying overnight."

"Yes my Lord," said the sentry, "follow me."

He led them into the castle where they came to an entrance hall with a staircase leading to other floors in the building. Two more sentries guarded the stairs. The first sentry spoke to one of the other sentries explaining who his visitors were and that they wished to see Sir Geoffrey on the Queen's business. On hearing this he spoke to Sir Ivor,

"If you will wait here I will enquire if My Lord will see you,"

"Tell him I am Sir Ivor his former student and that we carry the Queen's seal."

"Yes Sir Ivor," he answered. Turning he made his way up the staircase and out of sight. A few minutes' later two knights appeared at the top of the stairs and beckoned them to go up; they led them along a short corridor to a room where Sir Geoffrey was laid in his bed.

"I am Sir John, first knight to Sir Geoffrey, please come this way. My Lord is gravely ill from a wound he received at Lincoln. His end is nigh, so please keep your visit short, for I fear he will not last the night."

As they entered, even though the priest who stood by the bed was burning incense, the smell told them that the wound was gangrenous. Ivor went over to the bed.

"Sir Geoffrey, you old villain, what have you done too yourself?" he asked. Sir Geoffrey tried hard to lift his arm to greet Ivor but was too weak.

"Lie still, do not strain yourself old friend," continued Ivor. "We are here to collect your prisoner and escort him back to the Queen. He is to be exchanged for the King. We carry the Queen's ring, as proof to you of our quest." Toby stepped forward to show the ring. "I am sure you will be pleased to be rid of him."

"Good to see you again Ivor," Sir Geoffrey's voice was hardly audible. "I am afraid our reunion is too late, my life is at an end. But it gives me great pleasure to see my favourite student is in the Queens favour. John will release Gloucester to you; I am glad that responsibility is now yours and not mine." His gaunt frame sank deeper into the bed.

"You sleep in peace now Sir Geoffrey," answered Ivor, "you have earned the right, your legacy lives on in the knights you have trained. You will never be forgotten." Sir Geoffrey smiled, sank even lower into his bed, with a sigh as though relieved, he peacefully passed away.

The priest, who was now standing silently at the foot of the bed, moved closer and started to pray.

"It was as though he was waiting to pass on his prisoner, before he could move on from this world," uttered Sir John. "A lesser man would not have lived so long. It was as if he knew you were coming; I must make arrangements for his funeral, but first I must let his family know. I will tell Sir George to deliver the prisoner to you."

"Thank you Sir John. I am sorry I cannot stay to be with you at the funeral, but we must escort Sir Robert to the Queen without delay. Sir Geoffrey would have understood, I have yet to meet a man of his equal either here in England or in France. He will be missed," declared Ivor.

"Will Sir George be riding with us, or if not, have you men that can ride with us as escort to Sir Robert? There are those who would free him, harm him or kill him before we reach Winchester," said Toby.

"Sir George will go with you and eight others who are already guarding Sir Robert; they are no longer needed here. After all they are part of the Queens personal guard. They will then stay with the Queen whilst ever they are needed. He will find rooms for you tonight and ready your horses for tomorrow, food for your journey will be in your packs."

"Thank you Sir John for your generosity, we have not slept in a bed for some time," replied Ivor. They left the room and Sir George led them to the dining hall where they were well fed and then to rooms where they would sleep.

After an early night and a sound sleep, they were woken before dawn by a bang on each door and a cry of 'Breakfast is served in the main hall'. They dressed and made their way to the dining hall once more where they were met by Sir George, he was a well built young man of the same age as Tobias. He introduced the rest of the knights who would form the escort to their prisoner. After the introductions they all ate a hearty breakfast. The horses where saddled and ready for the journey. Sir Robert was brought up from the dungeon and tied to his horse.

"We must ride hard to reach Winchester on time," Sir Ivor told the men. "We eat in the saddle and stop only to rest the horses at midday and when the sun goes down."

They then mounted and left Rochester just as the sun cleared the horizon. Toby and Ivor led, sometimes at a canter, then so as not to tire the horses, slowed them down to a good walking pace. At night they stopped as soon as the sun went down, taking it in turn to stand guard for two hours at a time while the rest slept. Then moving on in the morning at daybreak. But this night Toby was uneasy in his mind. While the men were unsaddling their mounts he spoke to Ivor.

"Ivor, I am going ahead a mile or so on foot. If I am right, we should reach Winchester by mid-day tomorrow. I still think that sentry was too curious when we left there. If we are to be attacked it will be tonight or early in the morning, before they think we are ready for them, so keep a sharp look out and sleep in your chainmail just in case."

Toby slipped out quietly from the camp and moved stealthily down the road on which they were travelling. If they were to be ambushed, the perpetrators would have sent scouts ahead of the main party, sending word back to their comrades of how many were in the party they were about to attack, and where they were. Tobias was careful to keep in the shadows as he moved quickly down the track, but saw no one. He was cold and damp now, but just as he was about to turn and go back to camp, his sharp senses caught the faint smell of wood smoke. As he carried on, the smell grew stronger until he could see a faint glow of a fire in front of him. Quietly he moved forward but off the track now and into the cover of the forest, until he came to a camp in the clearing. Tobias counted six men sleeping round the fire, but could see no guards posted. The smell of horses made him move to his right, where he found two more men who were supposed to be guarding the horses, propped up against a tree, sleeping. There were eight horses tethered to a rope between two trees nearby, which told Tobias there were only eight men in total. Making his way to the far end of the tethered horses, he untied each horse as he moved down the rope, then he untied the rope from the tree furthest from the men and quietly moved away from the camp. Once out of earshot, he headed back to his own camp at a trot, partly to warm himself up, and partly to get to where he could now sleep until just before sunrise.

The next morning he woke the others early and told them what he had seen,

"They were all sleeping, there were no guards. If they are men come to take our prisoner, then they are not expecting us to have come this far." Toby told them, "I saw no markings on the men to tell who they were; they could be men searching the countryside for food, as they have done before, but we cannot take the chance. As I see it we have two choices, we can surround and attack them in their camp and find their intentions, or we can travel south a few miles through the forest, this way we skirt round them before turning west again toward Winchester."

"I think the latter may be best, yes we have more men, but we would have to leave men behind to guard Gloucester, and why look for trouble when we can avoid it," replied Ivor.

"Then we had better saddle our horses and move on before anyone finds us here. Pick up anything you have left. I want no sign we were ever here, no scraps of food, nothing." Toby told them. "Sir Charles and I will cover the horses' foot prints and remove the fire. Then when we are satisfied we have cleaned the area the best we are able, we will be your rear guard for a few miles. Try not to leave tracks for anyone to find, for the first mile at least, and don't let Gloucester leave any signs either."

Sir Ivor and the escort road out of camp leaving Toby and Charles to clean all the signs that would have shown that there was a camp there recently, and then follow the escort as rear guard.

There were no further incidents. Toby caught up with Ivor just as they arrived at the walls of the town, they rode through and up to the castle gates together. The same sentry came to meet them,

"Ere, I thought you were going home! Why have you returned? And who are all these men?"

"We missed seeing your ugly face! And these men, they are the best fighting men you will ever see, so I warn you not to trouble them." said Toby as he rode through and on to the castle steps, where they dismounted and pulled Gloucester from his horse,

"Sir George," Toby spoke. "When you take Sir Robert to the dungeons, only your men will guard him. Four of your men will be with him at all times. Under no circumstances let anyone near him, he speaks to no one no matter who they are, or how much they protest. You will not speak to him or him to you. Your men will take him his food and water, which they will bring from the kitchens themselves. He will be chained to the walls; two of the four guards will be locked inside his cell with him. Change the guard at meal times as they bring his meal. There are those who would kill Sir Robert, even here in the castle, so be on your guard at all times, for your lives are in danger too. Ivor, Charles and I will take our turn with you."

"I thought my time as a jailer was over," said Sir George, "we will do as you ask, Sir Tobias,"

The knights made their way up the steps and into the main entrance hall, where they were met by Sir William of Ypres and four of his knights.

"Have one of your knights show Sir George where Sir Robert is to be held," ordered Toby, "and if you would send another to tell the Queen's personal guard that Sir Tobias, Sir Ivor and Sir Charles have returned with the prisoner and wish an audience with the Queen, I would be obliged."

"Still giving orders I see," Sir William replied. "We will take the prisoner, and I will send word to the Queen that you have returned your work is done."

"I thought I was asking nicely. No . . . You will not take the prisoner Sir, he is in my charge. You Sir will stand aside, or have you learned nothing from our last meeting," Toby was now face to face with Sir William, "The Queen gave me my orders, and the Queen is the only one I will take orders from. Now do as I ask or stand aside." Ivor, Charles and the rest of the escort moved up behind Toby.

"My time will come Sir Rabbit Catcher, and when it does!" Sir William fumed, then, turning to his men, he ordered one to take the escort and prisoner to the dungeons and another to go and let the Queen know the prisoner had arrived and that Sir Tobias wished an audience with her. Sir William and the rest of his men left.

"That is twice you have made him back away Toby, be careful, he has powerful friends in high places," Ivor warned.

"I don't trust the man," said Toby. "How did he know so quickly that we had returned? The man on the gate must have had orders to let him know. And how did he know about the rabbit catcher part of my life? He must have been checking up on me, trying to find some dirt to smear my name no doubt." Toby replied. A knight came into the hall.

"The Queen will see you now, if you would follow me please." He led them to the same room from which the Queen sent them on their errand, where he asked them to wait. The trio did not have to wait long before the Queen came through the door at the far end of the room, accompanied by two Knights and Sir William of Ypres. The three knights bowed their heads in homage.

"You have made good time; I understand the prisoner has been secured in our dungeons, is he well? And Sir Geoffrey is he not with you?"

"Yes my Queen, Sir Robert, he has been well treated," replied Sir Ivor. "But I have grave news concerning Sir Geoffrey; on the day we arrived at Rochester, he died through injuries he sustained at the battle of Lincoln."

"Dead you say. Sir Geoffrey was a good and honest man, you would have to look far to find a man as loyal to the King as he. And the knights I left to guard Gloucester, what of them?" The Queen asked.

"Sir John stayed behind to organize the funeral; he will join us when he can. The other knights are here, on guard in the dungeon with orders to let no one near him. On our way back here, we came across eight men at arms camped on our path. As they wore no means of identification, we thought it prudent to go round them so as not to bring attention to ourselves. If they were a group looking for us, we thought our first duty was to guard the prisoner and make sure he came to no harm. But we will know them if they come here."

"Mmm, the exchange takes place in two days time. I charge you three and the knights which came with you from Rochester to guard him and keep him safe until the exchange. He is in your sole charge. After that the King will want to see you," replied the Queen. "You have served me well."

"If I may be so bold my Queen. First I would return your ring." interrupted Toby. The Queen took the ring.

"Secondly. With the sad loss of Sir Geoffrey as first knight to the King, I would suggest Sir John would make a good replacement. He also fought beside the King at Lincoln and was first knight to Sir Geoffrey."

"You may Tobias. Thank you for the return of the ring. I will put your suggestion to the King when he is free. Now you will take your leave of us, go to the dining room I have told the kitchen staff to prepare food for you all."

"Thank you my Queen," Toby answered as he turned and, with Ivor and Charles, left the room.

As they walked down the corridor toward the kitchen, Toby stopped, "I think we should go to see our prisoner and let our friend George and the knights eat first, while we stand guard,"

"You suspect something Toby?" inquired Ivor.

"I just have a feeling, nothing more," he answered.

"Could you not have these feelings after we have eaten?" asked Charles as they made their way down the stone staircase to the Dungeon. "I'm hungry."

"You are always hungry," was the simultaneous reply.

They turned and made their way deep beneath the castle to the dungeons. On entering they first found themselves in a large room. It was dark, lit only by candles and oil soaked torches giving off foul smelling odours. Instruments of torture were hung all around the cold stone walls, a forge stood in one corner, not unlike a blacksmiths forge which had bellows to pump air into it. It was lit, but the red embers gave a little warmth to the place. A feeling of desolation and despair came over Toby.

Three short corridors led off the room and at the entrance to one of them, stood Sir George and two of his knights, who appeared to be arguing with Sir William of Wpres.

"Is there a problem here?" Toby asked.

"This excuse for a knight is refusing to let me speak to the prisoner, me the Queen's right hand! I have the right to go anywhere in this castle including these dungeons while on the Queen's Business," answered Sir William.

"These men are guarding the prisoner on my orders. You were there when the Queen charged the three of us and the knights from Rochester to guard Sir Robert and keep him safe until he is exchanged for the King," replied Toby. "I see no reason for you to see the prisoner. While he is in my charge no one will see him, and so I would ask you to leave."

"The Queen will hear of this, you take too much on yourself, I will be back," he answered.

"And you will get the same answer, and if you are thinking of bringing men with you they want to be better than the ones you sent to waylay us in the forest," replied Toby.

"What! Are you saying I sent men to kill Sir Robert?" Sir William asked, "What possible reason would I have to do that?"

"No, not to kill him. Just to take him from us to show the Queen we are not competent to execute our task. But you were wrong, we did finish the task set for us, and we will finish the further task of keeping him alive and unharmed until he is exchanged for the King. You will not get the glory you seek here. Go and tell your tale to the Queen, but remember this, I saw the men you sent to waylay us; their horses have my mark on them. I will prove it was you who sent them," said Toby forcibly.

"This is not the end of the matter," screamed Sir William as he turned and left the dungeon.

The next two nights went without incident. It was now the day of the exchange. After breakfast, Toby went to the cell where Sir Robert was being held to make sure that he was clean and well dressed and ready for the occasion. A messenger came to tell Toby, Ivor and Charles, the Queen wished to speak with them. Leaving Sir George in charge with orders that no one was to see the prisoner, they followed the messenger to the Queen's quarters and into the room where they had met the Queen before, to wait on her pleasure. It was not long before the Queen came out to them; Toby and his friends fell on one knee and bowed their heads in homage.

"Get up, get up," the Queen told them. "You three have served me well, and have my thanks for your part in this. I am told Empress Maud is about to enter the castle grounds with the King. I want you to bring Gloucester up from the dungeon and meet me in the main hall where the exchange will take place. I will not have that woman in my sight any longer than is necessary. I will tell you when he is to be freed. After the exchange your mission is fulfilled, you three will come to the King's chambers and wait to see the King. Sir William of Ypres will escort Maud out of the castle."

"Sir Robert is ready my Queen, I will bring him up now, he will be under close guard until he is exchanged." Toby replied, and turned to leave. Charles and Ivor followed making their way back to the dudgeons.

They assembled the men in the large room at the entrance to the corridors where Toby spoke to them,

"I think we should have four knights to stay close to Sir Robert, along with us three," said Toby "the rest of you should be positioned each side of the hall watching for any treachery, both from Maud's men, and from our own ranks. What do you think Ivor?"

"That sounds fine to me Toby. You should be in front of Sir Robert, Charles and I behind him, with two knight's each side in close order." Ivor answered.

"Why from our own ranks," asked Charles.

"Because I don't trust Sir William. I don't think he would harm the King, but he may want to harm Gloucester," answered Toby, "Which would stir up more unrest and keep him in the King's favour. I am sure this exchange is not the end of England's troubles. Mark my words, unless Empress Maud is exiled and goes back to France and, while ever she has her general Lord Gloucester, she will be a thorn in King Stephens's side."

They brought Sir Robert up from the dungeons and into the Great Hall, where the Queen was waiting, she gestured to the guards on the door to allow Empress Maud and her escort guarding the King to enter.

"Bring forward the King that I can see that he has been well treated." The Queen ordered.

Empress Maud beckoned to her knights to bring the King forward. King Stephen looked ill, and was barely able to stand. Shaking with rage on seeing her husband in this state, she turned to Toby saying,

"Bring Gloucester forward and make the exchange, and then bring my husband to me," then turning back to Maud screamed, "I should have your head for this! But I must abide by the agreement I made. Take your brother and leave here as fast as you can before I change my mind and execute the both of you. In fact, get out of England, Stephen is King here! Sir William, take your knights and see them off before I change my mind."

Tobias and Ivor led Lord Gloucester across the hall, made the exchange and brought King Stephen back to his Queen.

"Come bring the King to his quarters, where he can bathe and have a meal," ordered the Queen, "I swear he has had neither in a long time."

The King was taken to his rooms by Tobias, Ivor and Charles, who, after seeing he was made comfortable, turned and asked the Queen for permission to leave.

"Wait one moment please," said the Queen, then turning to the King who was eating a meal of broth and bread that had been brought up from the kitchens, she spoke to him,

"These three knights have been very loyal to me and have worked hard in bringing about your release; I thought that you would like to thank them personally for putting their lives at considerable risk to have you freed from your prison." The Queen beckoned them forward,

"I recognize you, thank you Sir Ivor," said the King. "You were always a loyal knight, and one to be trusted, and these two knights you have with you, tell me who are they?" he asked.

"This is Sir Charles, knight to Gilbert de Clare, who has fought with you in the past Sire,"

"Yes I remember you too, my thanks to you Sir Charles." said the King.

"And Sir Tobias le Clerc, the lad you had me train as a knight at Nottingham Sire," he replied.

"Yes I remember you, the rabbit catcher. Sorry I could not be at your wedding but I was otherwise engaged. I hope everything went well, I will call on you the next time I am in Nottingham for a portion of that rabbit pie I was promised."

"My wife Lady Rebecca and I would be honoured Sire." said Toby.

"If it pleases my Lord, Sir Tobias has proved himself in battle, he was the knight who defeated and captured Gloucester. And then took the message to Empress Maud which secured your release and, though I was the senior knight, he like the born leader that he is, took charge in every way."

"That is how I remember your father Tobias, strong in battle and a leader of men. Now as I think I said at Nottingham, that part of my kingdom is safe. For your services to the Queen and I, as long as I am king you will pay no taxes, and you will be known as Sir Tobias le Clerc, Knight to the King, and put a rampant lion on your emblem opposite the rampant rabbit. You have been away from your young wife far too long, you have my permission to leave this place and go home with my eternal gratitude. If I need you in the future I will send for you."

"Thank you my liege, I will come whenever you need me, and gladly." Toby replied.

"And you Sir Ivor. You are already knight to the King. I would ask one thing of you, I would like you to consider training more young men in the ways of a knight, for we need men like Sir Tobias. What do you think? I will provide all the weapons and equipment you need, with a goodly sum each year from the kings purse. Will you do this for me?"

"Yes My Lord, I would be only too pleased. I now live in Nottingham with Sir Tobias and his family. If it pleases you to send the young men to me, I am sure that I can send them back fully trained in the ways of a knight, but it does take time."

"As long as you need, Sir Ivor, as long as you need. And you Sir Charles, I would have you known also as the King's Knight. You will attend me at court, and answer only to me and your Queen. Where I go you will go. I need a man that I can trust by my side, my eyes and ears. There are a lot of ladies at court, don't break too many hearts. You will also be paid from the King's purse."

"Thank you Sire, I will serve you well, that sounds just the type of work I have always wanted." Charles replied.

"Go now the King needs to bathe and rest, and my thanks for all you have done," interrupted the Queen. "I expect you will want to relax and get a good night's sleep before the two of you set off for Nottingham on the morrow."

"Yes my Queen," answered Tobias. "But before we go I would point out that the knights who have been guarding Gloucester these past months have lived in the dungeons like the prisoner they have been guarding. I think they should be rewarded too. Like Sir Ivor they are trained knights and will be an asset to you and the King."

"You have a way about you that I like, honest and straight forward, which is missing from the knights around me. I may call for you again. Yes they will be rewarded and kept in my service as the Queens Knights. Now go and let the King bathe in peace."

The three knights left the King to have his bath and went down to the stables. To make sure that their horses where rested and newly shod. For Toby and Ivor, that they were ready for the long journey before them.

They then found Sir George and his knights, to let them know that were to be kept in the service of the Queen and be known as the Queen's knights. The Queen would be sending for Sir George when the King was settled in his bed. They were well pleased.

"Now can we eat!" begged Charles.

"Yes." said Ivor, "I'm hungry too."

"Then forward to the kitchens and a hefty meal. Said Toby."

"Don't you mean a hearty meal?" asked Charles.

"You have the heart, Ivan and I will have the rest of the pig" chuckled Toby. "That would be a hefty meal."

"And he is going to be the eyes and ears of the King!" laughed Ivor.

They made their way to the kitchens and asked the cook to serve them a meal fit for three King's knights, and to make them a parcel of food to take with them as they travelled north the next day.

They rested the remainder of the day, before retiring early to the stables and a bed made of hay.

The next day at the crack of dawn Toby and Ivor said goodbye to Charles, and made their way north toward Nottingham. Each with thoughts of home and family. Ivor felt for the first time he had a family to return to. Toby, of his reunion with Rebecca and his mother. He was also feeling pleased that at last he had won his spurs and, earned the right to be called knight, a King's knight, like his father before him. And what both he and Ivor had achieved in the time they had been away. And how they together like brothers, had played their part to free the King from his enemies and put him back on the throne of England. But longing mostly for the peace that Sherwood gives to him and his family.

Long Live the King. And long live Farnsfield Manor and all who dwell there.

THE END